Crewel Yule

Needlecraft Mysteries by Monica Ferris

CREWEL WORLD
FRAMED IN LACE
A STICH IN TIME
UNRAVELED SLEEVE
A MURDEROUS YARN
HANGING BY A THREAD
CUTWORK
CREWEL YULE

Crewel Yule

Monica Ferris

BERKLEY PRIME CRIME, NEW YORK

A Berkley Prime Crime Book
Published by The Berkley Publishing Group,
a division of Penguin Group (USA) Inc.
375 Hudson Street
New York, New York 10014.

This book is an original publication of The Berkley Publishing Group.

First edition: October 2004

Berkley trade paperback ISBN: 0-425-19827-8

Library of Congress Cataloging-in-Publication Data

Ferris, Monica.
Crewel yule / Monica Ferris.
p. cm.
ISBN 0-425-19827-8
1. Devonshire, Betsy (Fictitious character)—Fiction. 2. Women
detectives—Tennessee—Nashville—Fiction. 3. Needleworkers—
Crimes against—Fiction. 4. Nashville (Tenn.)—Fiction.
5. Needlework—Fiction. I. Title.

PS3566.U47C74 2004
813'.6—dc22
2004054434

PRINTED IN THE UNITED STATES OF AMERICA

10 9 8 7 6 5 4 3 2 1

Acknowledgments

When the NMI Company invited me to their Nashville Market, I was thrilled. Every needlework shop owner goes to the various markets; I'd been told that from the start. But, since my needlework shop is imaginary, I thought I couldn't go. Not only did I learn a lot about shop owners there, but I also got the plot for this book. Thank you, especially Emily Castleberry!

And thank you Gail, my editor, who patiently found and plugged countless holes in the story.

Thanks also to Betsy Stinner, Marcia Kulik, Doug Kreinik, Dave Stott, Terrence Nolan, Frank and Judy Bialic, and several designers who kindly gave me permission to use their real names in this story. Everyone else is totally fictional, especially the suspects and the victim.

And thank you International Needlework Retailers Guild, sponsor of the Nashville Market.

One

Saturday, December 15, around 10:15 A.M.

Godwin, a slender, handsome young man in jeans and white cotton sweater, sipped his tea and looked around the atrium with happy interest. This was not his first trip to Nashville, but his first to the Nashville Needlework Market. As usual, it was being held at the Consulate Hotel; but not at all usual, it was being held in December.

Godwin didn't care, he adored shopping in any season and here was shopping squared: shopping for a shop. Namely, Crewel World, a sweet little needlework store in Minnesota, owned by his favorite boss, Betsy Devonshire.

Every year the International Needlework Retailers Guild

held a cash-and-carry market for member shop-owners, who came to select among the newest and/or most popular designers and manufacturers of needlework material. Not normally an early riser, he had been up and dressed, fed, watered, and ready for action as soon as the doors opened at nine, buying new and favorite counted cross-stitch patterns, new colors in fabrics and floss, new gadgets. Now, after carrying bags of loot out to the U-Haul trailer in the parking lot, he was taking a break to rest his feet and steady his nerves with a cup of tea. And, okay, a big chocolate chip cookie.

On one long side of the atrium were a restaurant—where he got the tea and cookie—and a bar, and on the other there was a swimming pool set up and a gift and notions shop. On the back end of the atrium was a warren of meeting rooms, while at the other, six steps led to a carpeted dais and three big double doors, through which was the lobby with its enormous Christmas tree.

Far overhead, the ceiling was nine stories away, and snow was building up on the glass roof. The snow had started last night and was continuing today. Who would have thought in southern Tennessee?

Surrounding the open air of the atrium, starting at the second floor, were tiers of galleries marked by painted iron railings ornamented with flower boxes from which descended thin cascades of ivy. And behind the galleries were comfortable little suites, each containing a bedroom facing the outdoors and a sitting room that faced the gallery. Starting on the second floor, and on through the sixth floor, every one of those suites was occupied by wholesalers who had packed their sitting rooms with needlework merchandise. Suites on the seventh to the ninth floor were held by those shop-owners who were first to register for the Market—Betsy Devonshire, his boss, was among them. Others had to make their slippery way to and from one of the motels down at the bottom of the steep hill on top of which sat the Consulate. That the Consulate was jammed with buyers was a comment on both the popularity of the Market and the tenacity of small business owners. And Godwin was carrying a Crewel World credit card. Heaven!

He took the last bite of his cookie and sipped his tea, which was still very warm and smelled of raspberries. Across the open floor, baby palms and flowering plants were set among small boulders that lined a miniature brook that curved diagonally across the tan tile floor. A little hump-backed bridge crossed the brook halfway along. A pair of white cockatoos fluttered and preened in their cage on the far side, near the foot of the stairs, where the brook ended in a tiny pool.

Godwin sat amid a scatter of wrought-iron chairs and glass-topped tables, most empty since breakfast was long over and it wasn't time yet for lunch. Godwin could hear a gush of women's voices from above and could have sworn he also heard a rustle of money or checks changing hands, credit cards being swooshed through little machines, and merchandise being pushed into plastic bags.

He opened the Market guidebook and began to plan his second foray. He'd done the sixth floor, so what was on four? He had the even floors, Betsy the odd. He'd heard Terrence Nolan was here. Sure enough, here was his trade name, Dimples. Suite 448—

A high-pitched sound pierced the cloud of chatter—a scream? A glimpse of something white falling, and the scream was cut off by a big, messy crunch down by the steps to the dais.

One of the birds screeched hard, and then human voices

began to shrill and shout. Godwin jumped to his feet, his knuckles hard against his mouth. That couldn't possibly have been—

But it was.

A *Tuesday in mid-August*

Betsy read the e-mail again and groaned softly. December was a very busy month. Crewel World would be open extra hours to accommodate last-minute shoppers, and there were preparations for inventory, and taxes, and the non-business tasks of Christmas, the rounds of parties—Betsy threw a big one herself for her friends and employees—all in addition to the usual long hours kept by any small business owner selling to the public, filled with stocking, doing payroll, cleaning, planning, and record keeping.

The e-mail explained that while International Needlework Retailers Guild normally held a cash-and-carry market every February, this year there was a glitch. Because of an error on the hotel's part, INRG had lost its February reservation. The Consulate Hotel was offering a free night' to the sellers and buyers of needlework materials—if they could come in December. Betsy had a reservation for February; would she be able to make the change?

No, December was impossible. Betsy clicked on Reply—and then changed her mind. The Nashville Market was very important. Shop-owners from across the country, including Betsy's rival shops in the Twin Cities, would be there, buying the newest patterns, the latest fabrics and threads, the most innovative gadgets. Regular customers might be disappointed if Betsy didn't go, and look elsewhere for consolation.

She asked her shop manager about it.

Godwin was adamant. "You have to go."

"I'd like to," Betsy said, "but you know as well as I do, December is the worst possible month for a buying trip."

At noon, her favorite employee, Shelly Donohue, came in. She was a school teacher who only worked full-time in the summer, but she was an expert counted cross-stitcher, and a patient, friendly sales clerk. Godwin would have gone out to lunch, but he took a few minutes to tell her about the change in dates for Nashville.

"Oh, rats, December is impossible!"

"See?" said Betsy to Godwin. "I told you we can't go."

Shelly said, "No, *I* can't go. Winter break from school won't have started, and I can't change the arrangements I made to take a long weekend in February." Betsy, having never gone to a market, had promised to take Shelly along when she signed up for Nashville Market.

"Well, how about taking me?" said Godwin. "This will be almost as much fun as NNA in January."

"Wait a second!" said Shelly. "That's not fair! You can't go to *two* markets!" Godwin had already agreed that he should go to the National Needlepoint Association Market in San Diego because he was an expert on needlepoint; counted cross-stitch was the focus in Nashville, Shelly's area of expertise.

He yielded gracefully. "You're right. So how about, just this once, we trade. We've both worked here long enough to know what our customers like in either kind."

"Hold on, you two," Betsy said. "I haven't said I'd go to Nashville yet. Adding thousands of dollars to inventory just before tax time is crazy."

"So don't open the bags," said Shelly.

Betsy blinked at her. "I don't understand."

"A long time ago, Margot ordered a whole lot of stuff from a supplier going out of business. She placed the order somewhere in the third week of December, thinking it would *maybe* arrive before the end of January. Well, UPS pulled up December 29. So she just stacked the boxes in her apartment and didn't bring them down until after inventory in January was finished." Betsy's sister Margot had been Crewel World's previous owner.

"Is that legal?" asked Godwin.

"I don't know," shrugged Shelly. "But Margot got the idea from another shop-owner who did the same thing. Neither one got into trouble over it with the IRS."

"That's probably because no one told the IRS about it," noted Godwin.

"And which of us three is going to say a word to the IRS?" demanded Shelly, staring hard at Godwin.

"Are you talking to *me*, girlfriend?" said Godwin, placing an outraged spread of fingers on his chest. He turned to his boss. "Not a word shall escape my lips."

Shelly said, "So see?"

Before the discussion could continue, the door went *bing*, announcing a customer, and they quickly put on pleasant faces as they turned to greet her.

"Hi, Jill!" said Betsy cheerfully—Jill was a close friend as well as a skilled needleworker. "Those Madeira silks you wanted came in this morning, I was going to call you."

Sergeant Jill Cross Larson, tall and athletic in her summer-weight blue uniform stood still a moment, inhaling the conditioned air as if hunting down a scent—or perhaps merely enjoying the coolness of it. Though the police building was only a few blocks away, it was very hot and humid outdoors. She had a habit of standing with her chin lifted and her eyebrows raised, a pose that always seemed to express mild doubt about the situation presented to her. It was probably mere habit, but it tended to make miscreants think twice about lying to her.

Jill was very fair. When she took off her six-pointed hat she revealed long cornsilk hair pulled up into a flat coronet of braid.

"Hello, Shelly, Goddy. Betsy, I want some more of that cherry-red wool, too." She started toward the triple row of wooden pegs on the long wall that held the thin skeins of needlepoint wool, then, identifying the scent, paused to look again at the trio and say, "What's the problem here?"

"Oh, the Nashville Market lost its site for next February and they've moved it back to this December. We've been talking about whether we'll go or not," Betsy said.

"No," said Godwin. "We're talking about who gets to go with Betsy, me or Shelly."

"No, that's settled," said Shelly. "I'm going to San Diego, you're going to Nashville. Gosh, California in January!" Betsy could almost see the Pacific waves rolling and crashing in Shelly's eyes.

Jill said, "When in December?"

"When in December what?" Betsy asked.

"What dates in December are you going to Nashville?"

"*If* I go, the fourteenth through the sixteenth. Anyhow, much as I would love to have you along, no one who isn't an owner or employee of a needlework shop can get into the Nashville Market."

"Hey, that's not why I'm asking," said Jill, faintly shocked that Betsy would think she was asking for a dishonest favor.

"There's a seminar on police management in Nashville in December I'm thinking of attending. It's the fifteenth, sixteenth and seventeenth."

"Hurrah!" cheered Godwin. "We can meet for an evening out. Are you anywhere near the Grand Ole Opry?"

Jill smiled and said, "This seminar is at the Grand Ole Opry Hotel."

"Oh, my *God*!" exclaimed Godwin. "Oh, Jill, you go right back to the police station and sign up! You *don't* want to miss this! Betsy, you have to see this place! It's as big as the Mall of America, but it's a *hotel*! It's got a *river* running through the middle of it! And there's a *jungle*, with orchids and palm trees! *Big* palm trees! And a New Orleans section, with jazz bands and—well, you just *have* to see it!"

"Looks like we're for it, Betsy," Jill said.

And Betsy surrendered, lifted her hands and said, "I guess so. I'll confirm our reservations tonight, Goddy."

Wednesday, December 12, 8.40 A.M.

Betsy and Godwin climbed into Betsy's big Buick with the next-to-smallest U-Haul trailer fastened behind. The trailer was there because the market was "cash-and-carry," meaning the thousands of dollars in stock they would buy must be taken away on the spot. And because neither Godwin nor Betsy traveled light, the backseat and trunk of the car were already filled with their suitcases.

Godwin had suggested Jill ride down with him and Betsy, but Jill couldn't spare the travel time, and so was flying down Friday morning. Which, as it turned out, was a good thing for her.

The temperature climbed as Betsy and Godwin drove

south, of course, and she felt comfortable sharing the driving with Godwin. But overcast skies turned to snow in Rockford, Illinois, and then to sleet. Betsy took over the wheel as sole proprietor, and they stopped in Bloomington for the night.

The sleet froze on contact with anything on the ground. The ice closed everything for most of the next morning, then the freeways opened. They took I-74 to Champaign-Urbana, then I-57 most of the rest of the way south. The ice melted and as they started seeing signs for Carbondale, Betsy began to feel optimistic and let Godwin drive again. This lasted until the landscape started to climb. By the time they rode I-24 into the corner of Kentucky they needed to cross to enter Tennessee, the ice was back. And Betsy was driving again.

Godwin, aware she was getting very tired, protested, but his car back home was a bathtub-size Miata and Betsy's big Buick had the trailer to complicate steering and stopping. She stopped for a six-pack of Lemon Diet Pepsi, and drank deeply.

Sleet turned back to snow. Cars filled the ditches and tangled messily on the highways. Betsy, a good winter driver, managed to avoid having an accident, but the delay was vexing. It was late Friday afternoon before they came into Nashville, and though the precipitation had turned back to rain, she was still driving and worn to a frazzle.

Godwin read the directions to the hotel off the INRG Market Nashville brochure and after bypassing most of downtown, they found themselves climbing a very steep hill in a series of switchbacks. THE CONSULATE read a sign in front of a big pink building at the top.

Betsy let Godwin out under the portico with the luggage and then very carefully chose a parking space she could pull forward out of. She'd had an embarrassing experience trying to back the trailer out of a parking space yesterday and was not anxious to see if she could make it work on a second try.

It was nearly dark on that rainy Friday evening before she pulled the key from the ignition. They were seven hours behind her most pessimistic estimated time of arrival.

The lobby of the Consulate Hotel was broad and gleaming, careful lighting marking the the check-in counter and seating areas while leaving the corners in dim, friendly shadows. Recorded guitars harmonized on "Silver Bells."

Godwin was leaning on the shining wood counter, filling out their registration cards, a wheeled cart piled with their suitcases behind him. There were two clusters of couches nearly filled with women talking and stitching. Against the wall opposite the check-in desk was a long table behind which women were handing out name tags and packets of information about the Market. Little Christmas trees and menorahs ornamented the table, and a huge Christmas tree nearly covered one of a trio of tall doors leading to the inward spaces.

Betsy looked at the women stitchers and sighed. She and Godwin had missed all the classes. Friday was for classes on stitching techniques, finishing techniques, and staying out of the red in the needlework business. She had really wanted to attend the classes on the last given by Susan Greening Davis and Betsy Stinner.

She went to present her credit card. She and Godwin were sharing a suite, since the original arrangement was with Shelly, and there was not another suite available. Then they went to get the information packet and ID tags.

"I'm sorry we missed Davis and Skinner," said Godwin.

"It doesn't matter," said Betsy, "I would've been too tired

to pay attention anyhow. Is the food any good here at the hotel? I don't want to go out again tonight."

"You'd better stay in," the woman said. "This rain is supposed to turn to snow, and Nashville just shuts down when it snows. Which it hardly ever does, so that's why. But they run a very good kitchen here."

Godwin, as parched as Betsy was hungry, said, "I'd settle for stale pretzels if they come with a beer."

"You're Miss Devonshire?" asked the desk clerk. "Here's a message for you."

It was from Jill: *Call me as soon as you get in. Let me buy you dinner here at my hotel. Goddy was right.*

"Right about what?"

"The fabulousness of the Grand Ole Opry Hotel, of course," said Godwin, suddenly looking much fresher, reading over her shoulder. "Let's get up to our room and dial that number. Do you like Cajun food?"

Two

Saturday, December 15, 10:21 A.M.

Marveen Harrison, night manager of the Consulate, was a tall woman of sturdy build and brisk, cheerful manner. But she blinked slowly at the cold gray light pouring in through the big windows and double door to the portico. She could see the white shapes of snow-covered cars beyond it, and yet more snow twirling down in large, beautiful flakes, coating the leaves on the trees—some trees stayed green year round in Nashville. It was beautiful—but strange.

Marveen had been night manager for over a year, and had gotten unused to natural light at work. She should be snuggling down to sleep about now in her heavily draped bedroom. But there had been an ice storm yesterday, followed by snow last night, and it was still snowing this morning. While she had made it to work yesterday evening, barely, she wasn't about to go out there again until the streets were clear—and, of course, the day manager had called to say there was no way he was coming in.

So pour me another cup of coffee, she thought, with a little lift of confidence, *I can do this.* She'd sometimes wished for an emergency that would prove her value and capabilities to the Consulate's owners. And here it was, with a vengeance. It had been busy yesterday evening with late arrivals—Midwest airports had been closed most of yesterday, delaying flights—and cancellations by guests unable to get there at all. Unfortunately, more guests managed to arrive than could leave, so she had four women camped in the big ballroom, using an old couch, a lounge chair, and two rollaway beds; and three men in the small ballroom with an inflatable mattress and two sleeping bags supplied by other guests. Fortunately, there were showers in the swimming pool complex they could use.

It was coming up on ten-thirty, and Marveen was checking the employee list to see who was here and who wasn't. They were going to be operating seriously short-staffed, all right. This would have to happen on a weekend when they were more than fully booked. Chef Brian Selph was here, that was one blessing; but the head of maintenance wasn't, nor was her lead housekeeper. Kayesha was next senior housekeeper, she would do—

The sound of a descending scream interrupted her planning. It cut off as something big hit the atrium floor. One of the birds started to shriek, and then people joined in. There were shouts of alarm, too.

Marveen froze. Her mind tried running in all directions, but every direction was blocked by denial. That couldn't be what it sounded like.

When she first came to work at the Consulate, she'd been concerned that there was only a railing between the guests walking in the halls—*galleries* was the correct term, but she thought of them as halls—and the great open space of the atrium. Suppose someone fell over a railing, and came smashing down on that hard tile floor? she'd asked. Couldn't happen, she'd been told. No way.

"Oh, my God," she murmured, keeping her voice down only with an enormous effort. She just stood there a few seconds, trying to remember how to breathe, listening to her heart knocking on her breastbone really hard.

Then her training and experience kicked in. She picked up the desk phone—and put it down again. She couldn't call anyone yet because she didn't know for sure what had happened, or how bad it was. Maybe it was a big old suitcase. Maybe it was only a broken leg.

Those thoughts gave her hope. She came out from behind the counter and hurried, reluctantly, to see.

There were three sets of doors leading from the lobby into the atrium. The one on the left was blocked by a huge Christmas tree, the one on the right led to a ramp for wheelchairs. The center doors were always open and Marveen stopped short just through them. Right at the foot of the carpeted steps was a solid mass of people all looking at something, all talking at once. Marveen heard words like *awful,* and *ambulance,* and even *dead.* She gathered herself and, starting down the stairs, asked in her most authoritarian voice, "What happened here?"

"She fell," said a woman in a pink fleece jogging suit.

"From the top floor," added a woman in a deep red sweater with a pattern of white snowflakes on it.

"I saw the whole thing," said a third, an older woman whose navy knit slacks were stretched to their limit over her tummy and thighs. "I was on the elevator and I saw her way up there, looking over the railing. Then she just went over and . . ." She touched her lips in a tentative way, apologizing with her eyes, clearing her throat as if to dislodge the words stuck there.

Marveen reached out to touch her on the arm. "Could you do me a really big favor and wait for me over by the front desk? I want to talk to you."

"Hr-um. Hem. All right."

Marveen turned and used her height and voice to make her way through the crowd. There was a little clear space in the center. No one wanted to touch the body, which was a body, all right—a woman. The inside border of the crowd was boiling like a pot. People wanted to see. Then they wanted to get away from the sight. As they went away, they were replaced by others who wanted to see, and then didn't. Marveen forced her attention away from the boiling to the body.

She had once seen a deer that had been hit by a big truck. That was what she looked like. Blood on a white sweater and broken bones in red slacks and blank eyes over an open mouth. Oh horrible, oh Jesus have mercy on that poor soul. Marveen looked away. But then she steeled herself and looked again, more closely. The woman was in her late thirties, maybe. Her hair was a bright blond. She wore one of those clear plastic card holders the people running the stitching event issued. It had twisted several times on its black elastic cord, but was, thank you, Jesus, face up. BELLE

HAMMERMILL, it read. BELLE'S SAMPLERS AND MORE, MIL-
WAUKEE, WI.

Marveen straightened and pushed her way back through
the crowd, then ran to the front of the check-in desk,
snatched up the phone, and dialed 911.

Thursday, December 13, 4:17 P.M.

Lenore was packing, her mind running on a well-worn track.
Belle deserves to die. She should fall off a cliff. She should
drink poison. She should go swimming where sharks can rip
her into pieces and eat her down to her toenails. She should
be hit by a train, which should back up and run over her
again, just to be sure.

Lenore could not believe she could hate someone this
way—but she did. Belle was evil. She loved doing wrong,
hurting people, ruining their lives. She was the worst person on earth; she was wicked, a devil.

"Sorry about that," she'd say, but she wouldn't lift a finger to make it right. "Sorry about that," with her sickening
smirk, but she wasn't sorry. She bragged to her friends about
how lazy she was, about how she was always messing up orders, forgetting it was her turn to open early or stay late.
"I guess I must be the silliest girl to ever own her own business," she'd say and actually giggle, like it was something to
be proud of. Cow.

But now Lenore's chance at becoming a successful designer,
at making a living doing what she loved, was destroyed,
smashed to ruins, and Belle, smiling, shrugging, was "sorry
about that," too. As if Lenore would get another chance like
this. As if Lenore should smile and shrug back, as if Belle
deserved to keep on shrugging, being sorry—or breathing.

It all began when Lenore started fooling around with a piece of dark teal Cashel linen. She was thinking of making a sampler, yes, a holiday sampler in reds and gold. Use Kreinik metallics, seed beading, Soi Cristale silk, and yes, Rainbow Gallery's Precious Metals Mini-garland.

But if it was a holiday sampler, then not done on the usual rectangle, no. Cut out into a Christmas tree shape—no, wait, done three-dimensional! Cut out, yes, and laced onto cardboard stiffeners—no, *stuffed.* Like a slender pillow, only in parts, eight parts or maybe even twelve parts. And it would stand up when assembled, a table centerpiece. A Christmas tree centerpiece for the holiday table, all sparkly and twinkly.

And keep the sampler idea. Ornament it with samples of fancy stitching: Hardanger stitches, counted cross-stitches over one and two, Rhodes stitches, star stitches, satin stitch, feather stitch, French knots, bullion stitch, even surface embroidery. And couching the gold mini-garland, some of it draped from pointed branch to pointed branch. Oh, happy days, oh, beautiful!

Weeks of planning followed. Go for a realistic tree, or pull out all the stops and make it a showpiece of fancy stitches? Bigger work on the bottom, tiny work on top? Try out this, practice that on doodle cloth, and even so, lots of frogging on the actual model. Blood, sweat, and tears. It became an obsession, but it was going to be fabulous; it would be a huge hit. Lenore described her idea and showed one section to a few stitcher friends, who didn't squeal and shout but made soft, awed sounds. And hinted that they would be honored, truly honored, to have a go at a section, pretty, pretty please?

Lenore sent a sketch and the stitched section to Bewitching Stitches, who immediately offered to buy it. And said they wanted the pattern to be introduced, with a model to display, at the Nashville INRG Market in February. And the money they offered was very, very nice.

Lenore started working on a new and better model of the piece. This one would be professionally finished—Lenore was a stitcher, not a seamstress. Like most stitchers, when it came to the washing, blocking, and framing, or the stuffing and sewing of a piece, she was barely competent. If she made a serious mistake, there were hundreds of hours of work spoiled. Besides, this important piece needed to be perfect. Good finishers were costly, but Lenore decided this piece would really have to be finished right.

She continued working on her practice model, correcting her pattern as things changed. All the while, her excitement level stayed high. It would be even more beautiful than she thought. This was going to be the design that gave her a name to remember.

And then a curt e-mail from International Needlework Retailers Guild:

> You have a reservation to attend next year's February Nashville Market. Due to a booking mistake on the part of the Consulate Hotel in Nashville, the February Market has been cancelled. The hotel, in an attempt to make things right, has offered us the second weekend of this December with one night's free stay. Please let us know as soon as possible if you can change your plans and attend the Nashville Market this December 14–17.

Could she make the new deadline? No choice—she had to. Actually, it would be better to have her new design introduced this December rather than the following February. The last time she showed the piece in progress, at a needlework guild meeting, a rival designer who had been lurking in the back of the room had left with a gleam in her eye, and Lenore's good friend Jeanne had said, "You watch, she'll have a pattern of her own that looks a whole lot like yours in six months."

Any designer who comes up with something new will find imitators. But the designer who had it first gets the undivided attention of pattern publishers for any designs she may dream up thereafter.

So Lenore labored hard on the practice piece. At last it was finished. She stitched, stuffed and assembled it herself. The fabric was roughened and distorted here and there from all the frogging—rip it, rip it!—of stitches as she changed her mind after seeing how they looked on the cloth. And because she wasn't a tailor, the assembly wasn't perfect; for one thing, it sagged to one side a little. And the stuffing was not evenly distributed inside all the sections. Yet, flawed as the finishing was, anyone could see how truly magnificent it could be, if it were professionally finished.

So she started in again. This time she just followed the re-worked pattern, so the stitching went rapidly.

Now, the only question was, could Belle Hammermill's finisher get it ready in time?

Belle said, "Certainly, no problem." The witch. The lying, lazy, slattern. The incompetent, wicked, corrupt, evil, stupid slut.

The day before Lenore was supposed to leave for Nashville, she went to Belle's Sampler Shop, and Belle acted all surprised that Lenore actually expected to pick up the design. Well, no, it wasn't ready. It wouldn't be ready until February seventh—wasn't that when Lenore asked to pick it up?

Lenore had been too astonished to get angry. Lenore had

talked to Belle about the change in the date of the Nashville market back in August; she had told her again when she brought the piece in, back just before Halloween, that she was going to introduce her newest design at the Market. She had even called the shop around Thanksgiving to remind Belle that the new date of the Market was just over three weeks away.

"Yes, I know," Belle had said. "Cherry and I are signed up. We're going to have a big sale when we get back."

But when Lenore went to pick up her model, Belle had said, with that cute little shrug she was a little too fond of, "Well, isn't that just too stupid of me? I guess I forgot to write the new due date down. Your model isn : here. Sorry about that."

No, someone like Belle needed to die. Die in some grotesque, painful way.

Three

Friday, December 14, 7:27 P.M.

Betsy wanted badly to tell Jill she was too tired to be good company, but Godwin was beaming with eagerness. So she called and said, "We'll be waiting in the lobby."

Jill came in a black rental Sable. As predicted, the rain had turned to sleet, and the twenty-minute trip to the Grand Ole Opry Hotel was an exercise in driving on streets and highways full of icy patches.

As they drove into the immense parking lot, Betsy looked at the acres of white clapboard building with various pillar-marked entrances and asked, "Is the hotel in a mall?"

"No, this *is* the hotel," Jill said. "Well, there are stores

and a canal and a park and buildings inside, but they're surrounded by hotel rooms."

"I bet the entire population of Excelsior could stay in one
wing of this place."

They parked and got out. The temperature had dropped,
and there was a brisk, cutting wind that hurried them up
the aisle toward the nearest entrance. Though it wasn't quite
snowing yet, the sleet was thickening with the promise
of it.

"I thought Tennessee was in the South," complained Betsy,
pulling her raincoat's collar closed around her neck. Godwin,
behind her, hunched his shoulders and shoved his hands
into the pockets of his beautiful camel-hair coat.

"I hear there are frost warnings as far south as central
Florida," said Jill, comfortable in just a Norwegian sweater
and knit cap. But Jill didn't put a coat on until the ther-
mometer dropped below zero.

The entrance they were heading toward was glowing with
thousands of fairy lights on tall shrubs. The shrubs were
iced over, blurring the pinpricks of light into a single glowing mass, very pretty. But Betsy didn't slow to appreciate the
scene. She pulled one of the wide double doors open by its
highly-polished brass handle and stepped into the warmth of
a broad hallway filled with the sounds of caroling.

The walls were lined with displays of fresh pine trees decorated for Christmas, and the air was sharp with their scent.
Jill came in behind Betsy and the three stood a moment,
while Betsy unclenched her shoulders and unbuttoned her
raincoat. Jill and Betsy were fond of Christmas. Both grew up
in homes where Christmas trees were real, and just the scent
set off a Niagara of nostalgia. Godwin noted the arrangement

with his artisan's eye and pronounced it a bit over the top, "just like it should be."

Jill made a face at him, pulled her cap off, said "Come on," and led the way down the corridor.

At its end they walked into a totally different climate. Though the air was still filled with the music of Christmas, it was also moist and heavy with the scents of earth, flowers, and tropical plants. A high earthen bank was set with stones and blooming plants. Betsy looked up and up and up. Mighty palm trees growing from the top of the bank made gentle parentheses around a space three and four stories high—and there was open air above them.

"Oh, my," she murmured, as she craned her neck.

"Told ya," said Godwin, inhaling happily.

Jill turned left, and they set off down a broad walkway that descended gently. On their right the bank continued. On their left were small verandas in front of what looked like row houses a door and one window wide. There were balconies on the second and third and fourth and . . . again Betsy's eyes went up and up. Wreaths decorated the doors, and candles were in all the windows.

"Oh," she said. "Are these the hotel rooms?"

"This is one neighborhood of them," said Jill.

They walked for awhile, then the path curved into an opening in the earthen bank to cross a bridge over a canal wide enough for two rowboats to pass one another easily. Fairy lights twinkled on the bridge railings and statues of carolers stood in little groups under old-fashioned street-lights along the canal bank.

"Isn't it romantic?" sighed Godwin.

The canal wound away under another bridge before it

vanished from sight behind more plantings. Another different set of apartment-like hotel rooms rose on either side and
still more were glimpsed beyond the trees in the distance.
"How big *is* this place?" Betsy wondered aloud.

"Beats me," said Jill. "I'd have to live here for a month to
really learn my way around. Come on, the New Orleans section is this way." She started up a walkway bordering the
canal. Betsy took off her raincoat, Godwin shed his overcoat,
then rehung it carefully over his shoulders.

Several walkways came together in a complex of arches
over the canal and on the other side was a broad street lined
with shops that offered dolls and teddy bears, or collectibles,
or candy. One seemed to be a kind of old-fashioned general
store. The shops were actual buildings, with roofs and chim-
neys, two stories high. On the sidewalk was a popcorn
vendor with a wheeled cart; the scent evoked summer even
more than the flowers and shrubs. Around the corner was a
small, cobblestone square with the canal—or maybe a different canal—on one side of it, and on the far side were
more buildings, pale gray stucco on their blank sides, heavily ornamented with wrought iron on their fronts. From one
came the hot, stirring sounds of a jazz trumpet. The canal
ran around back and on the other side of it was a sloping
bank covered with small trees and flowers in front of still
more hotel rooms. Betsy remarked, "While I love jazz, I'd
hate to be a really tired traveler who got assigned one of these
rooms."

"They do some kind of trick with acoustics. Once you're
more than twenty yards from the place, you can't hear the
music," said Godwin.

Betsy nodded. She hadn't heard the music until she came
around the corner. A neat trick, that. She wondered if it could

be applied to outdoor construction. What a gift that would be! But it probably required a specially designed roof over the whole area, like here.

The scent of highly-spiced food was also coming from the building with the jazz trumpet, and Betsy's mouth watered. "I hope this is where you're taking us," she said.

"Sure," said Jill.

The music was even better than the food, and they stayed late to listen.

Their minds were still on the hot, lazy feel of New Orleans when they came out of the Grand Ole Opry Hotel into the shock of winter. Real winter, now. Snow was coming down so hard they couldn't see more than a few yards ahead. It had piled up three inches deep, but there was no sign a plow had been through. Under the snow was ice, and they found themselves sliding helplessly into one another and the backs of parked cars as they blundered up the aisle.

"What kind of car are we looking for?" asked Betsy, who had forgotten.

"A black, four-door Sable," said Jill. "Rental plates."

Betsy chuckled. It was dark and all the cars were so heavily coated with snow it was almost impossible to see their color. Their license plates were covered as well—not that it mattered, Betsy had no idea how to identify rental car license plates.

"It was somewhere around here," said Jill at last, stopping to peer around. Betsy wondered how she could possibly know that. But when Jill took the keys from her pocket and pressed a button, a car only a few yards away honked and its tail lights flashed. "There it is."

An excellent driver, Jill nonetheless drove very gingerly out of the parking lot. She had the wipers going and the defroster on full blast. The headlights barely penetrated the heavy swirl of snow ahead of them.

"Maybe you shouldn't take us back," said Betsy, as the car slithered out onto the street—which hadn't been cleaned off, either. "We can double up with you, or get another room and go back in the morning."

"No," said Jill, after a moment. "No telling if this will be any easier tomorrow, and I don't want to be out here with a lot of traffic."

There was almost no one else out right now, the natives being nobody's fools.

Jill, by keeping her speed under twenty and starting to brake half a block early, was able to stop at a red light.

"This is scary," remarked Godwin, the first time the normally-chatty man had spoken since they left the parking lot.

"Are you sure we should continue?" asked Betsy. She glanced over to see Jill purse her lips and shrug her shoulders slightly to work out the tension. She looked back in time to see the light turn green. Jill gave it the Minnesota pause (Minnesota drivers, among the most dangerous in the country, take a traffic light's turning yellow as an invitation to floor it), and then took another three seconds to gain traction.

A few blocks later, an intersection offered a light which was already green, and Jill, having gotten up to a grand eighteen miles an hour didn't slow. They had gotten barely halfway through when a pickup, traveling helplessly sideways, its driver showing them his appalled, gape-mouthed face, hit her front right fender a glancing blow with his own front bumper. With a horrible *bang* the Sable's airbags inflated. Powder filled the air inside the passenger compartment as their car spun completely around. The bags began to collapse immediately and Jill, anxious not to be struck again, drove out of the intersection in the direction from which she'd come.

She pulled up to the curb and said, "Everyone all right?"

"I think so," said Godwin from the backseat. "Yes, all present and accounted for. Except my tummy's bruised."

"I'm all right," said Betsy after taking a few seconds to hear reports from distant limbs. "Are you?"

"Yes." They got out and Betsy went with Godwin to see how bad the damage was.

"Wow," he said, looking at the seriously crumpled fender and smashed headlight.

"But we're not leaking steam or oil," Betsy pointed out. The engine purred quietly behind the cracked grille, and the tire under the damaged fender seemed fine.

"Where's Jill gone to?"

Betsy turned around, peering through the thick snow. "There she is."

Jill had gone back to the intersection to look for the pickup, which had also spun around and was now resting against the curb facing the way it had come. The driver, a stocky young man, was slipping and sliding through the snow toward Jill, his eyes still very wide. Betsy and Godwin went to stand beside Jill.

"Are you all right?" he asked breathlessly. "I am *soooo* sorry! I hit my brakes but the car just ignored it. Are any of y'alls hurt?"

"No, we're okay," said Jill. "Are you hurt?"

"No, ma' am."

"Good. May I see your driver's license, please?"

This was said so crisply, the young man frowned at her. "I beg y'all's pardon?"

"Sorry, force of habit. Back home I'm a police officer. I hope you're insured?"

"Oh, sweet Jesus, a cop. Yes, ma'am, I'm insured."

They exchanged identification and insurance information. Jill made careful notes and the young man, seeing her do so, went back to his car for a notebook so he could do likewise. Betsy felt her feet getting wet and cold, so she went back to the Sable.

Jill and Godwin joined her a few minutes later. "Jill," began Betsy.

"I think we're closer to your place than mine," said Jill.

They were, though not by much. And the Consulate was at the top of a very steep, winding road. The Sable tried, and Jill was good, but at last she wrestled it to the side and set the front wheel tread firmly against the curb. "I'm afraid we have to walk from here."

"And you're staying with me tonight," said Betsy. "These people have no idea how to drive in this stuff, and I couldn't stand it if you got into another accident trying to get back to your place."

"I was going to ask to stay if you didn't offer."

They stopped at the check-in counter to get Jill a room. But the night clerk, a tall black woman with a kind voice, said they were full. "The couch in your suite pulls out into a bed," she said.

Jill said, "I'll take it."

"No, I'll take it," said Godwin. "Girls of a feather and all that."

Betsy registered Jill as a third party and the night clerk, on looking at Betsy's credit card said, "There's an envelope for you."

Betsy opened it in the glass-sided elevator going up to

nine. It was a slim booklet of eight-and-a-half by eleven paper with a plastic comb binding on one side. The front cover read "Management and Hiring" and was ornamented with a round gold sticker with EARTH THREADS and BETSY C. STINNER printed on it in black letters.

"Oh, this must be the handout from one of the classes we missed!" said Betsy. "How nice of her to get it to me."

She flipped through the booklet, which consisted of lists of rules stated in simple language and printed in bold type. Picking one at random, she read, "Never ever put off a problem. Problems put off only tend to get larger. Get to the root." Well, that was true enough.

The night clerk had given Jill an emergency kit of toothbrush, toothpaste, comb, and deodorant. Betsy had brought a nightgown as well as pajamas, so she loaned Jill the former.

But tired as everyone was, they were too shaken by the ride back from the Grand Ole Opry Hotel to go right to bed. They sat up and watched the Weather Channel exclaim over the massive winter storm that had stalled over the Midwest. Airports were closed from Denver to Indianapolis, and from Chicago to Nashville.

Godwin, gorgeous in magenta silk pajamas and matching robe, said, "Good thing we came back when we did, Boss, or we'd never get to spend a dime at the Market." He added, to Jill, "I'll bring you some catalog sheets tomorrow and you can pick out some stuff. We'll let you buy it for whatever they sell it to us for."

"Thanks," Jill said. "Maybe they'll have the main streets plowed by tomorrow afternoon and I can get back to my hotel."

Godwin snorted. "You've got to be kidding. This is the south, darlin'. There's a probably not a for-real snow plow in the whole city. When it snows, everyone stays home till it melts, which it usually does the next day. They get maybe one snowfall a winter, and *never* anything like this."

Jill looked at the window. "What, never?"

Godwin, on cue, sang the HMS Pinafore captain's reply, "Well, hardly ev-ER!"

Betsy shut off the television and they went to bed.

Four

Saturday, December 15, 10:20 A.M.

"She got me twice, Dave," Kreinik said. He was a tall, trimly-built man with a receding hairline of dark and coarse curly hair, owner of Kreinik Manufacturing, which made metallics, blending filaments and other fibers for stitchers. "First, she placed an order for all the sizes and colors of my metallics, COD. No problem with her before, so we filled it. When it arrived, she asked the UPS man to wait a minute; then she went into a back room, opened the box and took out the order and tossed in some trash, resealed the box, marked it 'Refused' and gave it back to the UPS man. By the time we figured out what she'd done, she'd placed—and quote *refused* unquote—a big order for blending filaments with the same trick. Last time I talked to her, she tried to argue it was a mistake on my end. It was a mistake, all right, and it happened when we shipped her that second order."

"Who did you say this person is?" asked Dave Stott, a round-headed man with a short-cropped beard. He asked the question in a quiet voice, as they were in the Kreinik suite, and there were customers present. But he wanted to know. Dave was the owner of Norden Crafts and didn't want to get caught by the same trickster.

"Her name's Belle Hammermill. She's from Milwaukee, owns a store called Belle's Samplers. You know her?"

"Never heard of her." Dave sounded relieved.

"You want an introduction? She came to the Market."

Stott, a short-legged man on crutches, snorted in disbelief. "You're kidding. She had to know Kreinik Manufacturing would have a suite here. What are you going to do, Doug?"

"For one thing, I'm telling this story to every supplier I can get to. She's going to find it damn hard in the future to place an order for other than cash in advance. But what I'd really like to do is confront her, call her a crook to her face. But a woman bold as that, who knows? She might punch me in the nose."

"Worse, she might—"

A sharp yell interrupted the pair, and Kreinik, facing the door, lifted his eyes in time to see something—someone?—fall past his vision out in the atrium. There was a dreadful sound of impact on the floor six stories below.

"What the devil?" exclaimed Dave, trying to turn too quickly on his crutches and nearly falling.

"Someone's gone over a railing!" Kreinik said as he pushed his way past Stott and headed for the gallery.

But the shorter man was right behind him, and they arrived at the railing together. "My God!" Stott shouted. "It's a woman! Oh, my God!"

There were shouts and screams from all over as Kreinik leaned out over the railing. "Holy cow!" He leaned a bit farther out, brushing against Dave, who could feel him trembling. "Who is it? Can you tell?" he asked.

"No." Dave leaned back awkwardly to look up. "Where was she standing?" The railings upward were dotted with staring faces—not many, because almost all the buyers and sellers were on the sixth floor or lower. The two men were six. There were none at all on the top floor right above her.

Kreinik grabbed the railing and shook it hard, but it was firmly attached. It was higher than his waist. His face was pale with shock, but his voice was calm as he remarked, "She must've been tall."

Stott wasn't tall, but he backed away one step before looking down at the people rushing to the railings on the lower floors. They were shouting and pointing, the great hollow space was filled with noise. And far below was a body, now surrounded by spectators. He looked away and said, trying to emulate Kreinik's apparent calm, "What—was she looking at something?"

Kreinik looked up, then shrugged. "I don't know. But it must have been an accident." He looked at Dave. "You going down?"

"Uh, no. In fact, I better get back to my place, make sure they don't leave it unmanned." He turned away, limping on one leg. His suite was almost exactly diagonal from Kreinik's, but didn't directly overlook the atrium. He was hoping all three employees hadn't gone running out to gape over the railing, leaving his stock open to temptation.

He wondered who the victim was. It was no one he knew, he couldn't remember seeing a blonde in a white sweater and red slacks this morning. But he felt sick at heart for her and anyone who knew her.

And while he was about it, for the whole Market. This was a terrible thing to happen! It was an accident, of course . . . or was it? No, of course it was an accident. Had to be. Anything else was unthinkable.

Wednesday, December 12, 9:40 P.M.

Cherry put a second extra change of underwear in her suitcase—she tended to take more underwear on trips than basic needs would require. She was frightened by how angry and desperate she felt. She needed someone to talk to, and not someone who would sympathize with her plight but someone who knew the law regarding business partnerships and small business operations. She wanted out—no, she *had* to get out. There had to be a way to break this partnership. Her sanity depended on it.

Belle Hammermill was a smooth-tongued liar. And their store, Belle's Samplers and More, was leaking money, melting money, *hemorrhaging* money. Cherry's money—and that was the Big Rub, wasn't it? Belle brought the expertise, Cherry brought the money, a perfect match.

Except it wasn't.

Cherry wasn't ordinarily a trusting sort; she'd had that knocked out of her by her first husband and his amazing family. But Belle was a sweet person, charming and funny. And really smart. She'd worked in retail all her life, and for the last four years in a needlework shop. So what wasn't to like, and trust?

And Cherry wanted to put a chunk of her money to work on an idea of her own—and herself, too. She had gotten a heck of a settlement from the city's insurance company after her accident. Which wasn't exactly hard. During rush hour a city bus had caught her in a pedestrian walkway and mashed her into a squad car. Broke her left elbow, left tibia and the sixth cervical vertebra in her spine. Tore the cord without severing it, so after some therapy she had control of her sphincter and bladder and could tell when something touched her legs—though, oddly, she couldn't feel pain in them. She could wiggle her toes and move her left foot, but she couldn't stand, except in chest-deep water. She was far from helpless: she had two lovely wheelchairs to get around in. She could swim, run wheelchair marathons, and drive her nice van anywhere with its hand controls. Above the waist she was perfectly healthy—in fact, her upper body strength was considerable—and her brain worked just fine, thank you. She had developed a particular dislike of people who saw her in a wheelchair and assumed she was a drooling idiot.

But she'd been taken good by Belle Hammermill. And the attorney she'd consulted said that there wasn't much she could do about it. The partnership contract they'd signed could be broken easily by mutual consent—but Belle liked things as they were, with Cherry continuing to pour money into the shop while Belle wasted it. And once Belle realized Cherry knew what was going on, her wastrel ways had become even more blatant.

So there had to be a way out. There just had to be. Cherry had money in other funds, but this was her first venture into hands-on investing and it was infuriating that she was being taken like this. If it continued, she was going to have to dip into other, secure, resources, and eventually she might find herself without the money to pay for the very expensive continuing therapy, or the new van she'd need in a year or two. Cherry knew a start-up business lost money its first few years and she was prepared for that; but Belle's Samplers had been bought as a going concern, and was now in its fourth year under her and Belle's management, and was deeper in the red than it had been its first.

Belle said it was because of the special requirements Cherry brought to the place, which was a steaming heap of bull dung. It was because Belle kept rotten records, took money out of the till, kept messing up special orders, and closed the shop whenever she felt like a day off. And she hinted to people that most of the shop's problems were Cherry's fault. But what could you expect when you took a cripple as a partner? When Cherry learned Belle had actually said that to a customer, she'd had to excuse herself to go into the bathroom and throw up. She had thought Belle was a friend!

This couldn't go on. Cherry had to find a way out.

Five

Saturday, December 15, 10:27 A.M.

The operator who answered after about a dozen rings sounded exasperated. "What is your emergency?" she demanded.

Marveen said, "We have a guest who fell into our atrium from one of the upper floors. She's dead."

In an oh-that's-different voice, the operator asked, "Who is this calling, please?"

"I'm Marveen Harrison, night manager at the Consulate at 7311 Harmony Drive."

"That one at the top of the hill?"

"Yes, I'm afraid so."

"Are you sure the person is dead?"

"Oh, yes, there is absolutely no doubt about that. We've got an eyewitness who saw her fall from the ninth floor. It's really terrible, she's a terrible mess, and she's really, obviously past any need for life support."

"Ohhh-kay. So not a life-and-death emergency. Which is good, all our emergency vehicles are out on calls, with other calls waiting. Your witness is sure it was an accident? She fell?"

Marveen glanced over at the woman, who was looking shaken but not excited or eager to garner the attention of a television reporter. "Yes."

"So you have no reason to think this is a homicide," the 911 operator was saying.

"Correct."

"I'll send a squad over as soon as one is available, but with the city streets so bad, I don't know how long it will be. Have you been able to clear the road up to your hotel for vehicle passage?"

"No, just the unloading area in front of the covered porch. We sent two of our maintenance people out this morning to shovel the parking lot, and one fell and sprained his wrist, and the other fell and hurt his back. It's terribly slippery out there." Marveen felt she was babbling and closed her mouth firmly while she took a breath. "But you will come, right? I mean, we have a situation here, a really, really horrible situation."

A tall blond woman wearing a winter coat over pajamas came into the lobby from outdoors and stopped to stamp snow off her slippers. Tried to use the stairs instead of the elevator, Marveen thought. Didn't realize you couldn't get to the lobby via the stairs.

"Have you got a place a helicopter can land?" The emergency operator's voice brought her attention back.

This question came up two years ago when a guest had had a heart attack. "Not really. I mean the parking lot is big enough, but it's full of cars; we have a full house. What isn't parking lot is hotel and trees. And the roof isn't suitable, most of it is glass."

"Okay, I've put the call out. But we've got a huge backlog and the streets everywhere are really slick. I hope you can be patient with us."

"I can, I guess. But I don't know about our guests." Marveen hung up and turned to the heavyset woman in the navy stretch pants.

"I hate to keep you just standing there, but I need to inform my boss."

"Yes, all right," said the woman. But her voice was thin with stress, and she was wringing her hands as she looked over her shoulder at the crowd in the lobby. Down the stairs, all Marveen could see were heads, but she didn't see the blond one; the woman in the winter coat had apparently gone on past the crowd.

Marveen had to look up the emergency contact number for the owners of the hotel—a good sign, really, because it showed how rarely it got called. She had to persuade the answering service that this was a truly genuine emergency that could not be handled by giving a message to be forwarded to the unfortunate individual on duty this weekend. The answering service connected her directly; Marveen did not have to dial a new number.

"Mr. Singh? This is Marveen Harrison, night manager at the Consulate. We have had a serious incident here, and one of our guests is dead."

She explained the situation, concluding, "No, sir, I understand, I'll instruct my staff not to talk to reporters. But I can't restrict the guests, of course. No, sir, I don't think you need to try to get over here, I understand the city is about closed down and I've got things under control here, pretty much." She extracted a promise from Mr. Singh that he would let the rest of management know what was going on. With a little sigh, Marveen hung up.

The woman in the winter coat had come back and had taken the plump woman over to one of the couches. Marveen sighed again, for a different reason, and came out from behind the counter.

"Thank you for waiting," she said, to call her attention away from the blonde. She used her kindest voice. "May I ask your name?"

"Sure," she croaked, and cleared her throat. "I'm Samantha Wills, owner of The Silver Needle in Clarksville. This is Sergeant Jill Larson, a police officer from Minnesota."

Whoops, that was different. Marveen shifted immediately from thinking her a disorganized, nosy nut, to considering the possibility that she was dressed like this because she responded in a hurry to the emergency.

Sergeant Larson had gotten a thin pad of paper and a pen from somewhere, she lifted them in a kind of greeting. "I thought I'd start collecting information until the local police arrive."

"Great," said Marveen, only a little doubtfully. "But can I speak with Ms. Wills now?"

"Of course," said Sergeant Larson, stepping back, but not quite out of earshot.

Ms. Wills said, "This is my first Market. You don't always have this kind of thing happening here, do you? I mean, that railing arrangement made me nervous when I first saw it."

Marveen recognized the question as a need for reassurance. "No, of course not," she said lightly. "Never before, so far as I know."

"That's good. Do you know the woman's name? The one who fell?" She was looking scared maybe it was someone she knew.

Marveen replied, "She was wearing a name tag that said Belle Hammermill."

"I don't know her," Samantha said, relieved. "I noticed her because she was standing up there all alone, with her hands on the railing, looking down like she was the president or something." She cleared her throat and gestured.

Sergeant Larson was writing. Marveen hoped she was really a cop, she must remember to ask for identification later. There was a new noise from the atrium and all three of them looked over and saw two young men in black trousers and white shirts pushing wheeled screens across the atrium.

Good idea, thought Marveen, wondering who had ordered them. She looked back at Ms. Wills and asked, "She didn't look sad, or scared?"

Samantha thought hard, her round face clenching with the effort. "I don't remember that. Maybe I couldn't've told, she was kind of far away. Anyway, I wasn't paying close attention. I just noticed her up there and then . . . she was falling." Samantha swallowed and grimaced, her eyes suddenly sad.

"Well, when our police get here, they're going to want to talk to you. But the weather out there is making travel difficult, and there have been a lot of other accidents, too, so it may be awhile." She thought. "Look, there's no reason why you have to sit here till they come. Let me write your name and room number down."

"I don't want to go back to my room to wait, I'll go crazy. But I've got a cell phone." She fumbled into a belly bag and produced it.

"Well, then, that's fine. Can you give me the number?" Marveen noticed that Sergeant Larson wrote it down, too.

Friday, December 14, 8:56 A.M.

She doesn't know I'm here, Eve Suttle thought, as she hung her clothes in the closet of her suite. She thinks she'll never see me again. But I'm gonna get her back in a corner and punch her lights out. If she pretends she doesn't know why, I may strangle her. Because she knows why, and she needs to know it's time she got over herself. She thinks being cute means she can behave any way she wants. She thinks saying "I'm sorry" is the same thing as "This never happened, so erase all memory of it." She's a whore—no, she's worse than a whore—she's not doing it for the money but because she wants to hurt me.

Eve nodded, liking that explanation, and started in a re-play of all the hurtful things Belle had done to her, something she had done over and over for months. She nurtured her anger with the painful memories, and she liked to keep it burning bright. Belle always expected people to forgive her, and usually they did. But this time she had gone too far—way too far.

Eve started by remembering when Belle was her friend. She had been happy working for Belle in her shop. With her humorous approach to everything, Belle made work fun. And she had seemed both generous and kind. When Eve made a mistake, Belle was quick to forgive her, and when Belle made a mistake, she had a cute way of admitting and even exaggerating it, which made you laugh and get over being annoyed, even when she did it over and over.

Eve had at first thought Belle's worst fault was forgetfulness. "Oh, my brain's a sieve!" Belle would say. "I'd forget my head if it wasn't fastened on!" And her customers would laugh and forgive her for not sending in a special order. *Most* of the time. Lenore didn't forgive her that last time. Eve had a special feeling of kinship with Lenore. Because it wasn't forgetfulness with Lenore, it was something weird and much worse—a kind of sick envy. Belle had liked Lenore so long as Lenore was a struggling artist, but once she showed real promise, Belle couldn't handle it.

And it was the same with Eve. So long as Eve was a fat and plain woman with a sickly kid and no husband, Belle was her friend. She showed Eve how to be the loyal, competent employee, and in return Eve rescued her boss from one scrape after another. Eve was grateful and she thought Belle was, too. But being competent gave Eve the nerve to lose sixty pounds, get a new wardrobe, color her hair, and win a really handsome boyfriend. Which Eve was sure added up to make Belle jealous. Things started to turn sour about then at Belle's store. Eve wasn't praised for her competence anymore, and her smallest mistakes were noted—and loudly. Then one day Eve came in to work and she overheard Belle saying to a customer, not knowing she was there, "I'm so sorry. I know Eve was supposed to handle this, but I guess she forgot."

Eve hadn't forgotten, Belle had forgotten.

Belle apologized so strenuously for that she cried. "I've been working terribly hard lately, and I guess this customer was getting on my last nerve. But I shouldn't have said that, it was terribly unfair, and after you've been so helpful and loyal." By the time she had finished, she had Eve crying, too.

But now Eve was sure that wasn't the first time Belle had blamed a failure of her own on Eve, because it sure wasn't the last.

And it got worse after Eve married Jack. Belle became more distant, and her remarks about Eve's occasional need to take time off to take Norah to the pediatrician were sometimes unkind. This from a woman who closed the shop whenever she needed a "mental health" day!

Belle had flirted with Jack when he was just Eve's boyfriend, and she continued even after they married. "Oh, he's so handsome!" she'd said when Eve dared to remark on it. "I just have to flirt with him a little bit!"

Eve was yet to discover Belle's true depravity, her sense of entitlement, her depth of resentment at Eve's blossoming. It happened when Eve was visiting her husband at work and casually logged onto his e-mail account to send a message—and found a whole set of red-hot, lusty exchanges between him and Belle. Jack didn't deny it. He said Belle understood him in a way Eve didn't. Jack packed a bag and left home that night.

And Eve, four months pregnant with her second child, wept until, sick and frightened, she had a miscarriage.

She quit Belle's, of course, and even moved back to her home state of Georgia with Norah. People were kind, and they all thought she was doing fine and even had mostly gotten over Jack, especially when she got a job at another needlework shop.

But the truth was, she'd gone insane.

It was true, Eve knew it. She hadn't told anyone, and no one guessed. But if anyone had asked, she would have told them, and proudly. Being insane was like being given a gift, because it didn't hurt anymore. She was strong, and the hardening of her heart was a blessing. She didn't mourn the lost child, not when she had a real, live person to blame for it. A real, live person who could be made to pay.

Six

Saturday, December 15, 9:48 A.M.

BritStitch on the fifth floor featured British designers. To Betsey's eyes, all their patterns were different,
some dramatically so. One big model fairly leaped to her
attention. It was of sheep standing in a stone-walled field of
tall grass, with fields in the background. The fibers were
shaggy wool or fine silk and there was an attractive slapdash,
almost impressionistic, look to the pattern, rather than the
precise placements of cross-stitches. One of the three fields
in the background was freshly plowed, the rows indicated
by chain stitches; another was covered with young green
growth of satin stitch, and the third was a rough blend of

golden-browns, like wheat or oats after the combine has gone over them.

The branches of a tree bordering the pasture were tufted here and there with red and brown, as trees would be in late autumn after losing most of their leaves.

"Wow," breathed Betsy, not very originally. Then the penny dropped. "Why, it's *crewel!*" There were smaller landscapes done in similar style, including a ravishing brook-under-a-stone-bridge scene. Betsy went quickly from one to the next, smiling and smiling. "I thought nobody was designing crewel patterns anymore!"

A tall, thin man with a white mustache smiled back at her. "Rowandean do," he said with a British accent. "And we're proud to offer it. We even have Jacobean crewel." He gestured at a set of framed models done mostly in deep reds and royal blues, stylized stems of flowers with cross-hatching filling in the outline stitches. This was a style of needlework very popular in the seventeenth century.

Betsy was so pleased she bought two Jacobean patterns, and four of the big sheep kit, though its retail price of seventy-five dollars would give sticker shock to her counted cross-stitch customers and the blank outlines would bemuse her needlepoint stitchers who were used to detailed paintings on canvas. She bought three other kits, a winter scene, the stone bridge, and another version of sheep in a meadow. She also took a catalog so that if the patterns went well she could buy more. She made a note on the catalog to check the types of wool required for the patterns. She didn't want to find herself unable to supply her customers if the kits didn't have all the wool needed to redo unsatisfactory stitches. Betsy was herself a famous frogger—"rip it, rip it!" was her motto.

As she went out the door of the suite, merry laughter

caught her attention. Two men and three women, were standing near the railing. One of the men was bouncing up and down on his toes as he said rapidly, "Throw the ball, boss! Throw the ball! Throw the ball!" And the others laughed again.

One of the women said in a scratchy voice, "I'm sick of crackers, give me a walnut." And they laughed some more.

The man who wanted a ball thrown glanced over and saw Betsy. "It's all right, we're not crazy," he said. "We're trying out what it would be like if our pets could talk."

Betsy thought about her beautiful but fat and lazy cat Sophie, and said—in a low and furry voice—"Honey, peel me a mouse."

More laughter. One woman glanced at her name tag and said, "Say, I know you from RCTN! You're the one with the shop near Minneapolis; I helped you out one time when you wanted to know about freebies. I'm Judy Baker of Stitchin House in Moline, Illinois."

Betsy came forward, rearranging her purchases so she could put out a hand. "Hi, it's good to meet you. Thank you for your advice."

Judy said, "These are Mike, Kathy, Phil, Mary, and Jean."

"How do you do?" said Betsy, shaking hands all around. "Are you having a good market?"

The consensus was, not bad, not bad. Though it was strange to be here in December, it was definitely better than not holding the market at all. Reminded of the work they were there to do, the group broke apart. Betsy would have gone on her way, too, but first she wanted to check her Market Guide to see who else she wanted to see on this floor. Whiskey Creek was along here; Betsy loved their boxes. She closed the guide and would have turned away, but her gaze was caught upward by a woman standing against the railing on the top floor. She was a very fair blonde, wearing a big, loose-fitting white sweater, an eye-catching subject against the darker background of the hall behind her. There was an air about her, of chin-up arrogance perhaps, or even triumph. *She's like a queen greeting her people after an important victory,* thought Betsy.

The woman turned her head to the left, and suddenly her right hand slipped forward off the railing. To Betsy's horror, the woman kept going right on over, shoulder first. A scream broke from her, and her hands grabbed futilely at the ivy and then at the huge emptiness of the atrium as she fell.

Betsy gasped and her eyes fled upward. She would not, could not, look down. Up to the empty railing on nine, she fastened her eyes there, until the scream was cut off by a horrid smack.

Feeling weak in the knees, Betsy reached for the railing in front of her—no, no, no! She backed away from it, eyes closing. No.

But now everyone was shouting and running and she was afraid of standing there blind, so she opened her eyes. People were rushing in both directions along the hallway, or crowding in front of her to gape downward. The air was filled with an uproar of excited and frightened voices. Someone brushed her shoulder as he reached to point downward. "Oh, gosh, look at her!" But Betsy turned her head up and away.

And there was Jill. She was standing by the railing on the eighth floor, looking down—but Betsy wasn't going to look down. She kept looking at Jill until the impulse to drop her own gaze passed.

Then Betsy knew what she wanted, and she wanted it right now: to stand in the aura of Jill's strength. Jill wouldn't be wanting to break into screams, or tears; Jill would know what to do.

Betsy knew there were stairs, but what if they were strictly for emergencies? What if you could get into the stairwell but not out again until you were at the bottom, where the dead and broken woman was? No. She saw a pair of elevators down the gallery, not far away. She joined the current of people going that way.

A car took a long time to come, and when it did, it wanted to go down, so she had to let it depart and wait for one to come up. People were all around her, saying, "Did you see it?" "Did you see her?" "I did, it was *sickening!*" "Who is she?" "Is she dead?" "I saw her, she's *got* to be dead!" "How did it happen?" "Where's that elevator?" "Come on, let's walk down!" But Betsy clenched herself shut, and waited for an elevator to come, to take her up, out of this.

It did, finally, and she dashed in and punched the button for the eighth floor four or five times, then jittered from foot to foot while it rolled smoothly upward. She was almost surrounded by glass, but kept her eyes firmly on the twin doors until the elevator stopped and they slid open. The eighth floor seemed empty. Certainly Jill was not at the railing anymore.

Betsy hurried down the hall, around the corner, to her suite. There were big bay windows on either side of the door, with the door inset between them. She fumbled the card key into the slot. A little light blinked green and she opened the door, almost falling in her eagerness.

"Jill!" she called.

No answer.

"Jill! Where are you?"

But Jill was not in the room.

Betsy stripped her wrists of the plastic bag handles and dumped them on the floor near the window. There was already a heap of filled bags there. She frowned at them until she realized they must be Godwin's purchases.

She wondered where Godwin was. Had he gone down to the atrium? Surely not—he would wish to attend the scene of an ugly accident even less than she did.

Was he still shopping? Was *anyone* still shopping?

The room was too silent. Who knew what was happening out there? She went out to see. The hallway was still empty, but there was a lot of talking going on down in the atrium, she could hear it. No screams or shouts now.

Maybe, somehow, she wasn't dead. Could it be? Reluctantly, she went for a look. There was a big knot of people down there, all talking and gesturing. As she watched a little clearing began to grow and there was the woman on the floor, her limbs impossibly crooked. Betsy looked away, but it was too late; the image left its outline on her retina, a stain that was permanent.

Her gaze fled along the atrium floor—and there was Godwin! He was going toward a table whose single occupant was someone in a wheelchair. The woman appeared to be weeping, and Godwin was being sympathetic.

Sympathetic was something Betsy could do. She decided to join them. She turned and went down to the end of the gallery, then turned down the long side toward the elevators. Halfway along, sitting on the floor, was another weeping woman. She was in navy-blue slacks and sweater. Her knees were drawn up and her forehead was resting on them, and she was sobbing so hard her shoulders were shaking.

Betsy went to stoop beside her. "Here now, here now," she said, "are you all right?"

"Y-yes," the woman managed. She gulped and went on, "Or I will be. That poor woman, I saw her . . . on the floor down there . . . Oh, God, Belle's dead!" The sobs renewed themselves.

"Belle—was that her name?" asked Betsy. "Did you know her?"

The woman nodded. "I used, used to w-work for her. B-Belle Hammermill. Sh-she's from Milwau-k-kee." The woman wiped her face on her gabardine knees and sniffed once, twice. "Sor-sorry."

"Yes, it must be a shock to you, seeing someone you know . . . like that." Betsy touched her gently on the shoulder. There were lots of silver threads in the yarn of the dark sweater, harsh to the touch.

"A shock, yes. T-terrible." The woman lifted her face to look at Betsy and forced a trembling smile. Her oval face was surrounded by very curly auburn hair; she was pretty, or would be when she wasn't so upset. "Thank you for stopping," she said. She glanced at the name tag and added, "Ms. Devonshire." She choked and sniffed hard, seeking control. "Sorry. I'm Eve Suttle from Silver Threads in Savannah. But I used to work for Belle."

"Oh, then this must be especially horrible and sad."

Eve made a strange grimace. "It—is. I can't stop crying." She began a struggle to stand. "I'm sorry, making a nuisance and all."

Betsy helped her to her feet, concerned at the pale face, the glazed brown eyes. "I think you should go lie down, at least for awhile."

"Oh, no, I'll be all right. I'm supposed to be shopping for Silver Threads, and Mrs. Entwhistle will be upset with me if I don't get all the things on her list."

"I wouldn't worry about that right now. I think everyone's stopped buying until this gets sorted out. Here, let's go this way. Did you know Ms. Hammermill long?"

"Three years." Eve came along docilely. "But then things—well, I decided to move back home, to Savannah. That's where I'm from originally, and there I went to work for Mrs. Entwhistle. I have lots of family there, and they're helping me raise my little girl . . ." Her voice went high on the last two words, and she put her palm against her nose and mouth. "Sorry, sorry."

"Here, this has shaken you more than you know, I think," said Betsy. "What's your room number? I think you definitely need to lie down for a bit."

"We're down there, in seven twenty-three." The woman looked down the gallery.

"On seven? But this is eight!"

"It is? But the stairs went around twice . . ." Eve shook her head. "I was on the elevator, you see, and got off on the wrong floor."

Betsy frowned at this conflation of stairs and elevator, and Eve explained, "I was thinking about something else. So when I got off the elevator and went to my room, the card wouldn't work and then I realized I was on the wrong floor. And I came down the stairs, and . . . and then there was this scream and when I looked . . . Oh, my God!" She bent over as if her stomach had clenched tight. "My God."

Betsy put a hand on the back of her sparkly sweater and circled it slowly twice, a calming stroke. "Take it easy, everything will be all right. Come on, I'll walk you to your room."

Eve managed a faint, "You're being very nice, thank you."

As they started along the gallery, Betsy cast around in

her mind for something to say. Finally she asked, "Was Belle a good boss to work for?"

"Yes, at first. But then . . ." Eve swallowed and said rapidly, "But I got homesick, I guess. You know how it is." She made a gesture seeking understanding; but she didn't look at Betsy, and seemed to withdraw into herself, so Betsy politely didn't ask any more questions.

Seven

Saturday, December 15, 10:08 A.M.

Jill was stitching in Betsy's suite. Betsy had taken her down to the INRG desk in the lobby first thing this morning and explained that Jill had been trapped at the hotel last night by the snow, and so was not only without a change of clothes, but also the little stitching project she'd brought along to work on at idle moments during the law enforcement management seminar. Could she please buy a kit or something (she'd pay retail, of course) so she wouldn't have to sit twiddling her thumbs until the streets cleared?

They were generous—more than generous. They told her she could buy anything she wanted from any suite, at the same prices shop-owners were paying. They even gave her a special name tag so no one would question her right to shop. And they happily sold her an INRG T-shirt, too.

Jill waited until they were on the elevator back up to eight to remark that it was a pity INRG wasn't selling official Market underwear.

After breakfast, Jill had seen Betsy and Godwin off on their buying spree, then gone shopping for herself. In Connie Welch's suite she found a little kit with a Santa Claus face to be glued to a piece of stiff felt to which beads were added as ornament. No glue was included in the kit, so Jill made a side trip to the front desk, where the clerk found her a little bottle of Elmer's white glue. Jill used it on the spot, drizzling it on the back of the plaster head and pressing it onto the center of the white fabric. Then, partly because scissors weren't included in the kit, but mostly because Jill needed a new pair of scissors and wasn't averse to buying them at a wholesale price, she was pleased to acquire a beautiful little pair of Ginghers. And because she was allowed to buy anything, she could not resist a lovely Purrfect Spots pattern of a polar bear on a blue ground, its nose lifted up to sniff a red Christmas tree ornament hanging on a red ribbon. It was called Yukon Yule. Though she liked needlepoint best, Jill, like most stitchers, could do several kinds of needlework. And this pattern was lovely.

She started back to the elevator, but a suite that had needlepoint canvases caught her eye. J&J Designs was the name. The were printed rather than hand-painted, which meant their prices were reasonable. She paused to consider the beautiful Panda, a near-abstract, curved shapes of black on white, but bought the Measure Twice Cut Once canvas with its tiny models of tools and a frame for it taller on one side than the other, as if its maker had not followed the advice. Her husband would be amused.

She went back to the suite. Before she sat down to stitch she figured out how the windows operated and slid one open a few inches, then opened the door to the hall so a draft was created. Jill almost always found hotel rooms far too hot for her taste and had to find a way to lower the temperature about fifteen or twenty degrees. She had already changed out of her clothes back into the flimsy nightgown Betsy had loaned her so she could rinse out her underwear and also so she would not be tempted to return to the sales floors. Soon she was content in the fifty-eight degrees of chill she had created.

Also, she opened the door hoping the cleaning woman would come in. Or at least so Jill could hear her pushing her heavy cart and invite her in. No need to make her have to come back repeatedly to see if she could finish her assigned rooms.

By now the glue was dry on the Santa head. Jill trimmed the felt back close to the head, threaded the hair-like beading needle and made a quick circuit of the head on the felt with a single row of green and red beads. Then she consulted the instructions and did a row of picot beading—bring the needle up through the fabric, string three beads on the thread and go back down close enough to the first stitch so the middle bead is forced out, making a tiny, square loop. Repeat all the way around.

Jill had finished that and was stringing beads and tiny metal ornaments to make the first long string of fringe to hang down from the bottom of the Santa head when she heard a scream. By the time it was cut off, Jill was on her feet, and two seconds later she was out in the hall, looking over the railing.

On the tile floor below, right at the center foot of the carpeted stairs, Jill could see someone crumpled, limbs at impossible angles. The cockatoos in a cage near the body were shrieking, their noise nearly drowned in the shouts and yells of people rushing to the body.

She whirled and ran back into the suite. No robe, no time to dress—she grabbed her winter coat and shoved her toes into Betsy's slippers. They were too small, her heels hung over the backs.

She grabbed her purse by its strap and was out the door. She ran on long legs down the hall—not for the elevator. She went for the door back in a corner. The stairs.

Like most parts of a hotel rarely seen or used by guests, the stairwell was utilitarian: gray paint over steel steps, buff paint on the rough concrete walls. Her feet thundered as she raced down. She was not even breathing hard when she reached the bottom.

But the stairs decanted her into a hallway that led only outdoors. She opened the door into a blizzard. High winds and a thick whirl of snow batted at her. She started down a barely-visible narrow walk that was snow over ice. She passed a thin tree and noted how the snow clung to leaves—the trees had leaves! In December! The slippers had no grip, and, distracted, she fell. She staggered to her feet. But even scuffling along, she kept slipping and sliding, and once slid into a car, burying her hands above the wrists in snow on its hood.

She made her way as fast as she could down to the front of the hotel then up and under the portico, where the wind was blowing like a tornado, lifting her coat and nightgown indecently. Hands pushing down, she hurried to the front entrance, and inside the first set of doors she paused to stamp snow off her feet and resettle her coat. The nightgown clung to her knees and there was snow in her fair hair as she walked into the warmth of the big lobby.

Someone was saying into a phone, ". . . eyewitness who saw her fall from the ninth floor."

There were loud voices out in the atrium, she could hear them coming through the center open doors. They were coming from a crowd gathering around the body. But the lobby had only three people in it. One, a tall, stocky black woman, was behind the check-in counter. She was the woman who had given Jill the glue bottle—and, Jill realized—the clerk who had checked her in last night. She was talking on the phone.

". . . not breathing. She's really, obviously dead, past any need for life support," the woman was saying, talking to emergency services. That was good.

Standing near the twin couches was a very plump woman in stretch knit slacks who was staring anxiously at the woman on the phone. Probably the eyewitness. That was good, too, pulling her out of the crowd before her memory could be mixed with other people's.

And in a wheelchair behind the INRG check-in tables was a thin woman with a thick, smooth helmet of white hair. She wore a gray dress printed with big black leaves, and was talking on a cell phone while looking with alarm at the crowd in the atrium. "No, no, stay where you are, it's a madhouse here—and you couldn't get over here, anyway, the news is saying all the streets are impassable." Probably talking to another INRG official.

Jill strode past the counter into the atrium, down the steps and up to the crowd. "I'm a police officer, let me through," she announced. The people made room but slowly, staring at her, confused by the contradiction of the authority in her voice and the strange outfit she was wearing.

At the center, in a small clear space, lay the body. Definitely a body, not an injured person. She had beautiful light blond hair in a tangle of curls, an oversize sweater that was still mostly white, and red wool slacks. One low-heeled black shoe had come off but lay on its side beside her shattered foot. Near one shoulder lay a small purse, its contents spilling. A Market Guide, open and folded back, had suppliers marked in red—the red pencil itself was near the dead woman's hand. Jill looked up, but nowhere was the line of gallery railing broken. So why had she fallen over?

The crowd shifted as two employees pushed through, carrying a dark brown blanket they had already started to unfold.

"Hold it!" ordered Jill. "Let's keep the scene just as it is for now." The two men halted to look at her uncertainly. "I'm a police sergeant. Not from here," she added, "but the rules are the same." She reached into her purse and produced the folder with her ID card and gold badge. "My name is Jill Cross Larson."

The badge did it, the men brought the ends of the blanket back together and edged away through the crowd.

Jill looked around at the gapers, some of whom had stopped staring at the body to stare inquiringly at her. "I want a perimeter, all right?" said Jill, in a voice that left no room for discussion. But they didn't back up to enlarge the circle. She pointed to three strong-looking men and two tall women in the crowd. "You, you, you, you, you, come here." They obeyed. "It may take awhile for the police and an ambulance to get here," she told them quietly. "I want you to space yourselves out around here, facing the crowd, and keep anyone from approaching any closer. We don't need people tracking footprints all over the place. In fact, if you think you can, you might move them back a few feet."

The five looked quickly at one another. "All right," said the tallest one, a bald man with graying sideburns. He stepped away from Jill and stood facing the crowd, his arms held away from his body, palms front. "Everybody take one step back, if you can," he said in a loud, firm voice. "An ambulance is on its way."

The other four quickly followed his example of standing facing the crowd with their arms out, and they moved forward as the crowd edged back.

"Let me through!" a woman said, fighting the movement, and Jill turned to see a stout Hispanic woman in a red sweat suit waving at her. "I'm in law enforcement, too!" she added.

Jill moved to intercept her before she could break the line her volunteers were setting. "Thank you for speaking up," she said.

The woman squinted as she confessed in a murmur, "I'm just a part-time 911 operator back home, but they don't have to know that. Can I help?"

Jill smiled briefly. "Sure. See if you can find some hotel staff who can scare up five or six portable screens for us. It would be a good thing to get the victim out of sight and it will protect the scene. It looks like emergency services is going to take a while to arrive. Then we'll need someone to stay here, to keep people from sneaking a peek."

The woman nodded, then checked her watch. "I can stay about an hour, and then if I need to, I can arrange for a replacement."

"Thank you."

Jill went sideways through the crowd and back up the steps to the lobby. The black woman behind the counter was saying, "No, sir, I understand, I'll instruct the staff not to talk to reporters. But I can't restrict the guests, of course. No, sir, I don't think you need to try to get over here, I understand the city is about closed down and I've got things under control here, pretty much."

Talking to management, that also was good.

Jill walked up behind the plump woman, who was still staring at the woman on the phone. She touched her gently on the shoulder, and the woman gasped and turned sharply.

"I'm sorry to startle you," said Jill in her gentlest voice. "Do you know what happened?"

"Yes, I was in the elevator and I saw her fall. She was on the ninth floor and she just went over the railing."

"You're sure she fell? She didn't jump?"

"I saw her standing alone up there, looking over the railing. And then—over she went." The woman made a hump shape with one hand, and cleared her throat.

"Was she looking at something? Or at someone?"

"No—well, I don't think so. I thought she was just looking around. I did it, too, when I first came out of my room. Just stopped to look around."

"Was it an accident, her falling?"

"I don't know." She cleared her throat again. "Maybe . . . or maybe she did jump."

"You saw her, did she lean and fall, or climb over?"

"I—well, I don't know. I guess I looked away for a second."

"So you didn't actually see her fall."

The woman bridled a bit. "Yes, I did! I was riding down in the elevator from five, they're all glass and it's like a ride at a carnival. So I didn't turn and look at the doors, like you do in a regular elevator. I looked down, but it's kind of scary the way you see the floor coming up at you, so I went to looking up. And I saw her up there all alone, and then I saw her falling. And when I looked up again, there still wasn't anyone there."

Jill nodded. "All right, good. That's very clear, thank you."

Reassured, the woman smiled and relaxed.

"My name is Jill Cross Larson, and I'm a police sergeant from Excelsior, Minnesota. May I ask you some more questions?"

The woman's light blue eyes widened. "Okay."

"Excuse me just two seconds." Jill stepped to the far end of the check-in counter to pick up a ballpoint pen and two sheets of hotel stationery, which she folded twice on her way back to make a stiff little pad on which to write.

"May I ask your name?"

"I'm Samantha Wills, from Clarksville." Samantha coughed and said, "Hotel air, it makes my throat dry."

"Tennessee?" asked Jill, writing.

"Yes. I own The Silver Needle. I took it over from my aunt, who retired last year."

"Do you know who the victim is?"

"No. But she was up on the top floor, so I think she was a store-owner. The wholesalers don't have rooms up there, do they?"

"They're only selling things from the sixth floor down," said Jill.

"Yes, that's what I thought. This is my first market. But I didn't recognize her up there, and over there . . ." Samantha swallowed hard, and nodded toward the hubbub out in the atrium. "It's hard to say, now. I mean, she, she's kind of . . ." Suddenly her face crumpled up, and she put a hand to her forehead.

"Here," said Jill, "let's go over here where you can sit down. That wasn't a nice thing to see."

"It sure wasn't," the woman said sincerely.

Jill took her by an arm and led her to one of the pair of couches facing one another. "Are you all right? Do you need a drink of water?"

The woman shook her head. "No, I'm all right. Just a little scared, I guess. It was scary to see her fall like that. I've never seen anything like that before."

"I'm sure you haven't. Which elevator were you riding in?"

"That farther one, over on the pool side." She gestured with hand and head.

The woman who had been on the phone said, "Thank you for waiting," and they both turned to see her approaching. "What's your name?" she asked Samantha.

"I'm Samantha Wills, owner of The Silver Needle in Clarksville. This is Sergeant Jill Larson, a police officer from Minnesota."

The woman looked at Jill, obviously reworking her initial impression—crazy lady in a wet nightgown and too-small slippers. "I'm Marveen Harrison, Manager."

Jill held up the paper and pen and said, "I thought I'd start collecting information until the local police arrive."

"Great," said Marveen. Still, reluctant to give up any authority, she said, "But can I speak with Ms. Wills now?"

Jill nodded and stepped back, but prepared to write down anything more Samantha Wills might say.

Jill heard a rattle of wheels and glanced out into the

atrium. A young woman in dark slacks and white shirt was pushing a tall chrome frame whose center was filled with a dark, rust-brown fabric along the tile floor toward the crowd around the body. The Hispanic woman in red was walking with her, explaining something. Behind them was a young man, with another frame. Noisy buggers, everyone was looking. She hoped there were enough of the frames to make a perimeter.

Then she realized she was not thinking of this as a disturbing tragedy but a crime scene. Why should she do that?

Jill thought about the sturdy, ivy-covered railings, none of them broken through. So unless the victim was leaning way out for some reason, this probably was not an accident. Then she recalled that Market Guide, marked in red. People planning a suicide don't plan shopping trips.

That left murder. But Samantha said the victim was all alone up there. On the other hand, a single eyewitness was a fragile thread to hang an explanation on. Jill made a note: *Other eyewitnesses?* And under that Jill wrote the name of a person she trusted could find out the truth: *Betsy!*

Eight

Saturday, December 15, 10:23 A.M.

Cherry had heard the yell and the ugly sound of something landing on the atrium floor, but she didn't go look. She almost had second thoughts when people below started to scream, but resisted the urge to go gape like a yokel. Instead, she rolled down the middle of the hall, turned the corner, and continued toward the elevators. She pushed the call button. It took a little while—the elevators were very busy—but at last one came. There was only one person in it, and she moved out of Cherry's way only when Cherry brushed up against her. Her expression was perfectly calm.

"What's going on?" Cherry asked. "What's all the yelling?"

"I don't know," the woman said vacantly. She had that "shopper's hypnosis" stare, and she got out at six without saying anything else. More people got on, laden with plastic bags. Cherry hated crowded elevators, everyone standing so tall and close. It was like being in a well full of elbows.

Two women were talking about the beautiful charts in the Pegasus Originals suite. "So romantic," sighed one. But the other three squeezed past her to stare out and down through the glass walls of the elevator. "See it?" whispered one.

"God have mercy, I've never seen anything like that," said one from behind her hand.

"She's dead, she's got to be," murmured the third, and there was a horrified silence, as the Pegasus admirers turned to stare.

Cherry turned her chair just a little so she could look between fleece-covered elbows. She saw a golden-haired woman on the floor, her body flat, her limbs all wrong. She was surrounded by a fast-thickening wall of people staring or gesturing in alarm. Cherry's breath stopped until she looked away, and even then she had to force her diaphragm to operate.

The elevator stopped. Two women got off, three others managed to get on. The elevator went down. Cherry looked out and down again. The angle of her view of the atrium floor had changed. Now she mostly saw a big group of spectators.

"Do you know who it is?" asked one of the murmurers, still looking.

"No, do you?" replied another.

"No."

The elevator stopped at three and its doors opened. No one got off, so none of those waiting could get on. The doors shut on their disappointed faces.

Cherry looked out and down again, watching as a tall black woman pushed her way out of the crowd and ran up the carpeted stairs and into the lobby. Must be going to call an ambulance, or the police. Or both. Soon the place would be swarming with police and emergency medical techs.

The elevator moved downward. The dead woman was invisible behind the crowd, but Cherry knew who she was. She said nothing. She rode the elevator down to the ground floor, got off last and wheeled her chair up and over the little bridge across the miniature brook. She started to follow the others toward the crowd around the body, paused, then turned away and went down toward the glass tables and iron chairs. She stopped at the first table she came to, and put one clenched fist on the table. She heard a quiet sound of lament and lifted her head to look around before she realized it was coming from her.

How could she be sad? She hated Belle! But tears spilled from her eyes. That sight of her, broken like that, was too much, too awful.

A slender, blond-haired young man sat down across from her. He looked blurry through her tears. "Do you know who she was?" he asked, his voice as kind as it was curious.

She nodded. "Her name was Belle Hammermill. We were partners in a store in Milwaukee."

"Oh, my God, I'm so sorry," he said. He rose swiftly and went away, only to return seconds later with a handful of paper napkins. "This is all I could find," he said, putting them on the table in front of her.

"Thanks," she said, taking one and wiping her eyes. She took a second and blew her nose. They were the good, thick kind of napkins, soft as tissue.

"Can I get you anything else? A glass of water? There's someone in the bar, maybe I can get you a brandy."

She found herself smiling at him, even though her forehead was pinched by her eyebrows hiked upward and together. He had nice, old-fashioned manners, offering the two treatments old-fashioned men thought good for shock or loss.

To her surprise, she found the idea of a drink attractive. "Could you?" she asked him. "Brandy?"

"Certainly." He went away again.

She kept wiping and blowing, there seemed no end to it. She wondered who the man was. Maybe he was gay; gay men often had nice manners. He was back in two minutes with a little snifter of brown liquid. The taste was harsh, and it was very warm in her stomach. Amazingly, it almost immediately stopped the tears.

"Thank you," she said, dabbing at her nose.

"Do you want to go over there and talk to someone?"

"No." She was very sure about that.

"They may be wondering who she is," he said, but not unkindly, and he sat down.

A small detail of the body appeared in Cherry's mind. "She's wearing her name tag, they can get her name off that," she said. She put the glass down on the table with a too-hard clink. "Does that sound heartless?"

"Well . . ." He studied her for a moment. "More cowardly, I guess."

A sound almost like a laugh came out of her, surprising and frightening her. "I'm not a coward!" she declared. "But they'll make me look at her, and while I wasn't too fond of her lately, I don't want to do that. There's no way I could do that, I'd start screaming or throw up. Or both."

"I understand," he said. "I'm Godwin DuLac, by the way. From Excelsior, Minnesota."

"Cherry Pye," she said, "from Milwaukee, Wisconsin." She waited for the little look she always got when giving her name, but it didn't come. Probably already read it off my own tag, she thought.

"Can I ask you something?" he said.

She nodded, poised to explain her father's weird sense of humor.

"Was Belle upset about something? Or sad?"

Taken aback, she blinked, then said, "I don't think so. I mean, she didn't say anything to me. Why? Oh. . ." He was thinking Belle's death was a suicide. She took the rest of the brandy in a single small mouthful while she thought. "Well, she has been making more mistakes than usual."

"What kind of mistakes?"

"Ordering things and then sending them back. Forgetting to order things. Forgetting when it's her night to close up or her morning to open. She's always been a scatterbrain, but she's been worse lately. As if something's been on her mind. But she didn't act depressed, she just laughed it off like usual." Cherry thought some more. "I don't know, I've been so tied up with my own problems lately . . ." She hadn't meant to say that, she bit her lips and reached for the brandy, but the glass was empty.

"Do you want some more?" Godwin asked.

"No. No, thank you. That was nice of you, to think of it. It really helped." She looked over her shoulder. The crowd was noisy; everyone giving orders. "Will you stay with me for a little awhile? Just until I get the nerve to go over there?" Because she really must go over there.

"Of course," he said.

Nine

❧✿❧

❄ Lenore sat quietly on the small couch in Bewitching Stitches' suite. She wore a long, deep green, matte-silk skirt and a wine-colored blouse with bell sleeves. Her curly dark hair was in a loose arrangement on top of her head with tendrils that showed off her slender neck and delicate ears, and would have made her look sweet and vulnerable if she weren't already looking sullen and angry.

On a low, square table in front of her was the model of her Christmas tree sampler. There were two things right about it: the dark green Cashel linen it was made of—the same shade of green as her skirt—and the perfect, balanced placement of the various stitches. Everything else was wrong; most prominently, the dejected way it slumped on its base. But the roughened areas of the linen where stitches had been pulled out didn't help, and the hasty, almost clumsy way the eight parts had been sewn together was painfully evident. *Awful,* she thought, *how I can make a dozen perfect French knots in a row but can't piece a pattern?* No wonder people glanced at it, then went on by.

It did not occur to Lenore that it was still early in the buying period, or that customers saw the unhappy scowl on her face and kept on going.

"Here's the coffee you wanted, Lenore," said Vinny Moore, President of Bewitching Stitches, putting a Styrofoam cup of foamy café latté down in front of her. "And here, have a pastry, it will cheer you up," he added, holding out a paper plate with three fruit-filled selections.

Too deep in misery to get the hint, she shook her head and Mr. Moore retired to the other side of the room.

Lenore contemplated the stack of patterns gloomily. It was going on ten o'clock, and there had been a steady stream of customers through the suite. There had been a few sales, but not enough to lower the stack noticeably. Certainly not enough to qualify her pattern as a hit.

Lenore felt part of the problem was bad placement. She should be seated next to the check-out table, where people had to stand and wait while their orders were rung up. There, having nothing else to do, they'd take a closer look at the model. Then they would, perhaps, see past the snagged fabric and inadequate finishing to the clever design.

Or maybe it wouldn't help. Mr. Moore should know his business; maybe he looked at her model and just plumped her down here to sink or swim.

Lenore needed a big success here at the Market. The pattern deserved it, and good sales would mean they'd buy her next pattern, too. Her husband Coby stayed on as credit manager at Harley-Davidson because the pay was good and they offered great benefits, but the work was not challenging and he often talked of starting his own accounting firm. Now that Mike and Alyssa were both in school, her husband—not unjustifiably—wanted her to share the burden and find a full-time job. But if this new pattern led to regular work as a designer for Bewitching Stitches, her income could easily go higher than what she could earn as a full-time cashier at Pik n' Save.

Maybe she should have canceled her appearance in Nashville, and just taken a chance with Bewitching Stitches' catalog presentation. No, making a personal appearance—Meet The Designer!—was important, despite the cost of travel.

Well, then, maybe she should have left the crappy model at home. No, the pattern was complex and difficult, and it needed a model. A photograph or drawing wouldn't do. But this model . . . It was tooth-grindingly awful to have to put this thing on display. Oh, there had been a few customers who could see past the flaws, but most were just coming in long enough to buy patterns by known designers, and would only have paused if something brilliant caught their eye. Something like the properly finished model Belle had promised Lenore.

There ought to be a special place in hell for people who deliberately smash the dreams of others, thought Lenore savagely. *And Belle can't get there any too soon.*

Another customer came in, glanced very briefly at Lenore and her model, then turned away. It was a rejection so clear

Lenore nearly cried out in protest. But she stuffed it down, though the effort deepened her scowl.

Then her anger flared up even brighter at the injustice of it all. Wouldn't it be great to go find Belle? Lenore had seen her at breakfast, filling a plate with scrambled eggs in the buffet line, laughing and talking just as if she were not some kind of weird monster. Cherry wasn't with her. Lenore thought about that. Was the partnership in trouble? There was certainly some tension between Belle and Cherry. Lenore recalled the sudden silence that fell when she came in a week ago, and, once before that, Cherry turning away too late to hide her angry face. *Probably Belle's fault. No, undoubtedly Belle's fault! The witch.*

And here was Belle in Nashville, in easy reach. All by herself, Cherry wasn't with her.

But how to get away? Lenore, overwhelmed by a desire to escape, reached hastily for the Styrofoam cup of coffee on the little table. Her grip was awkward as she lifted it. She tried to rearrange her grasp without putting it down and managed to flip it into her lap.

Hot!

She jumped to her feet with a hiss, sending the cup bounding across the room and flipping brown liquid from her skirt all over the table. The patterns were in plastic bags—except the top one, which was for customers to peruse. And the model. The pattern was spattered—but the model was drenched.

Lenore gave a wordless yell and ran from the suite.

Saturday, December 15, 8:58 A.M.

Eve Suttle's employer said, in her charming Georgia accent, "Y' all' re better at samplers than I am; how about you buy

them? Here's your copy of my credit card. Please, *please* try
not to spend more than two hundred on sampler patterns."

"Yes, ma'am, Mrs. Entwhistle." Eve had grown up in Savannah, but had long ago lost her accent, if not her manners. She wasn't sure how to go about regaining it, or if she
should. Would it be reclaiming her roots or mocking them
to deliberately slow her words?

She wasn't going to have any problem limiting her purchases. Belle was here, Eve knew because she had asked at
the front desk last night and when the woman said yes, Eve
had left a note telling Belle when and where to meet her.

That meeting time was now in less than an hour; Eve was
anxious to be on her way so she could do enough shopping
to satisfy Mrs. Entwhistle and still make the meeting. She
had not, of course, told anyone about it. She took the card
and stowed it in an inner pocket of her purse, then checked
her watch.

"There's someone here with a sampler shaped like a
Christmas tree, see if you can find it," Mrs. Entwhistle said.

"Okay." It was ten after nine.

"Eve."

"Okay."

"Eve!"

"What?" Had she missed something? Eve was anxious
not to give away any hint that she was less than focused on
buying product for Silver Needle. "I'm sorry, I think I'm
not awake yet."

"See if you can find that sampler shaped like a Christmas
tree. I can't remember who is sponsoring her."

"Oh, that. I know the designer, if she's Lenore King from
Milwaukee. She used to come into that store I worked at up
there, to show the owner parts of her design. What I saw of

it looked really great, but I never saw the whole pattern. I'll look for her, and if her model's good, I'll be sure to buy a couple of patterns."

"If it's really good, buy half a dozen. All right, we're set. See you at lunch."

It was nearly time for the meeting when Eve passed through the Bewitching Stitches suite. Lenore King wasn't there, and her model looked as if someone had spilled something on it, cocoa or coffee. How awful, because Belle charged the earth for finishing. But wait, this model had problems besides the stains. This couldn't have been properly finished! How could Lenore put this out where people could see it? Sales of the piece must be suffering because the model looked so bad.

Eve stooped for a closer look. Actually, it was a really clever design—and they were coffee stains, she could smell it. She knew several people who would love to stitch something as beautiful—and difficult—as this, including herself.

She straightened. "Is this Lenore King's design?" she asked.

A man behind a little table said, "Yes. And that's only her working model. The real model wasn't ready on time for the Market, I guess because we got moved up two months."

Eve knew Lenore had been stitching a showcase model of this pattern months ago; there had been plenty of time to get it finished by mid-December. So it wasn't hard to guess whose fault it was the real model wasn't here.

Eve hid her anger at this further evidence of perfidy and looked around. "Where's Lenore?" she asked.

"She went to change her skirt. She upended a whole cup of coffee on herself," said the man, who was short and sporting a curly dark beard. "Do you know her?"

"I used to, back when I lived in Milwaukee. She was always coming up with nice sampler patterns, but this was her masterpiece, I remember how hard she was working on it. And if you give it a good look, you can see that it turned out *really beautiful*!" Eve said that last sentence nice and loud so other customers could hear her, and added, just as loudly, "I want six patterns of this beautiful Christmas tree sampler, please!"

She quickly chose a few other patterns so long as she was there, then hurried off to her ten o'clock appointment with Belle.

Saturday, December 15, 9:40 A.M.

Lenore was crying in fury and frustration as she shoved her door card into the lock on the ninth floor. She stripped off her beautiful silk skirt and panty hose in the bathroom and wiped her bare legs with a washcloth soaked in cold water. The skin was only a little red and there were no blisters, but her hands trembled with aftershock.

And when she looked in the mirror, she was further discouraged at her awful face. Her eye makeup was smudged and her nose and eyes were red. Her hair was hanging crazily—she had run her fingers through it on the elevator. People must have been staring at her, crying and dripping coffee and wiping her hands in her hair.

This was impossible. She couldn't go back down to Mr. Moore's suite. And why should she? He would have thrown the ruined model away by this point, surely. She couldn't sit there beside a stack of patterns with no model. *And looking like the crack of doom*, she added, again noting the ruins in the mirror.

She couldn't go home. No one could leave the hotel, the blizzard had all the streets and roads closed. What was she going to do for the rest of the show?

First of all, she closed the plug in the bathtub, put her stained skirt and panty hose in, and covered them with cold water. The stains hadn't set, maybe they could be rinsed out. Then she washed the smeared makeup off her face, let down the rest of her hair and combed it out, and changed into jeans and a chambray shirt. Now she looked presentable, and, except for the glow of fury in her eyes, totally different from the sullen artisan who had sat in Bewitching Stitches.

It was ten after ten when she decided to go look for Belle.

Ten

Saturday, December 15, 12:55 P.M.

The police hadn't come yet, so Belle's body still lay where it had fallen near the foot of the steps. It was surrounded now by screens made of seven-foot-tall stainless steel frames filled with brown cloth. A gray-haired woman in black sweats and silver lamé walking shoes sat on a folding chair outside one of the screens, eating soup and crackers from a bowl sitting on a plate. Everyone knew what the screens hid and she guarded, but knowing is not the same as experiencing. The atrium was full of only slightly-subdued voices talking and even laughing.

The hotel had set up a big, round table at the other end of the atrium, offering a buffet-style lunch of two kinds of soup plus chili, breads and crackers, and a salad bar. The restaurant in the far corner was open, with a full menu, and the bar was serving hamburgers, hot dogs, and cold sandwiches. Most of the glass-topped tables and chairs had been moved toward the center to make room for the buffet table. The ones nearest the buffet were thickly crowded, but diners thinned out the closer they were to the screens—though even the nearest was a dozen yards away.

"Why didn't they set up in the big ballroom?" asked the person ahead of Betsy in the buffet line, dipping into the chili pot.

"Because there are people camped in the big ballroom," said the person ahead of her. "And the small one. People who were supposed to check out this morning, but who can't get away because the airport's closed. Not that they could get to the airport, even if it was open," she added, lifting and tipping the metal bin that held the last of the grated cheese over her bowl. Betsy sighed. She would have liked some cheese on her own chili.

Since it was impossible to leave the hotel, everyone was eating in today, and extra chairs were brought from the smaller meeting rooms. And awful as it was to eat in the presence of death, people didn't want to be alone, so the bar and restaurant were packed and all the tables in the atrium were occupied, even the unpopular ones. Those who managed to get a place at a table near the buffet found they could quite literally rub elbows with their fellow diners.

Betsy stood bemused; she had been among the last to file

past the big round table with its picked-over greens and nearly-emptied dressing bins. She'd given up her desire for a salad and now, with a bowl of cheeseless chili and a glass of milk on her tray, she couldn't see a place to sit down. Well, she could have crowded in with the four oblivious people at the table *over there,* but not if there was any alternative.

Then she saw Godwin stand up and wave at her from a tiny round table meant for two that had Jill, another woman, and two other men sitting at it. Nevertheless, he gestured again for her to come over, pointing at an empty chair set a little to one side. As she approached, slowly and doubtfully, the others moved their chairs back, enlarging their circle to make room for her, though it meant they had to reach well forward to spoon or fork up a bite of their meals.

She smiled her apologies and said, "Thank you for making room." She sat, put her bowl on the table and began to crumble her crackers inside the packet before opening it and sprinkling them over her chili.

Godwin said, "I don't know why people won't take their food up to their rooms. This place is packed!"

"If you're feeling crowded, why don't you go up?" asked Jill, giving him one of her coolest looks.

"I don't know." He put his fork down and looked as if he were about to take her suggestion, but changed his mind. "Because I don't want to. What happened was so horrible, I don't want to be alone."

"See?" said Jill.

"Me, too," said Betsy. "It's awful to be so near . . . her, but I feel like I need to be around lots of people."

"Besides," said Godwin, "there's people here you want to talk to. When you're shopping, you're shopping. When you're eating lunch, you get to catch up with old friends." He looked around at the others at his table. "I'm Godwin DuLac, by the way. That's Betsy Devonshire, my boss, who owns Crewel World in Excelsior, Minnesota."

A small but very handsome man with dark hair and brown eyes sat across from Godwin. He was holding his turkey club sandwich in his hand to give others room on the table.

"I'm Terrence Nolan, I design for Dimples," he said. "I'm with you on not wanting to be alone."

"No, you *are* Dimples," Godwin said, and smiled to show his own dimple and waved his eyelashes at Terrence.

Terrence waved back, he even added a wink, and Godwin began to glow. With his lover John hundreds of miles away, Godwin was like a horse let loose after a month in the barn. A mere dead body wasn't going to stop him flirting.

Betsy said to Terrence, "I like your birds, especially Rex and Spike, the kingfishers; and I love the Santa heads. You make him look like a real person, kind of sad but kind. Not that I've stitched them," she added hastily, "but the models hanging on the wall of my shop sell a lot of your patterns."

"You need the eyes and fingers of a ten-year-old to stitch some of those patterns," agreed a good-looking man in a black sport coat and open-collar green shirt. He had a strong accent that put him from somewhere near New Jersey. His head was shaved entirely, an attempt to disguise his male pattern baldness, but the bald spot was outlined in a gray shadow. He touched his temple in a kind of salute.

"I'm Harry Mason, I own Hal's Floss and Fabric store in Philadelphia."

"You and your wife?" asked Godwin, hoping not and prepared to flirt in that direction, too.

"No," replied Harry, then dashed Godwin's hopes by continuing, "My wife is an attorney. I was an architect until I broke both legs in a car accident and was laid up for a long time. A nurse brought me a counted cross-stitch kit. I liked it so much that I asked for another, and by the time I was up and around I was hooked."

He looked to one side and asked in a southern accent, "How bad was you hooked, boy?" and replied in his Philadelphia accent, "So badly that I quit my job with Wolfe, Barnes, and Kirkwood to start Hal's Floss and Fabric, Inc. That was four years ago; and my goal in life is to show men how needlework can save your life, even your soul. It's not expensive, it's not hard to get started, but you never run out of things to learn about it. Plus, you can enter it in competitions." He looked away and said in that southern voice, "But Ah don' *lahk* competitions!" And went on in his normal voice, "Or not."

Godwin giggled and said, "Do you often talk to yourself?"

Harry raised his eyebrows and said with earnest curiosity, "Never! Why do you ask?"

Godwin laughed again and said, "Never mind, forget it. How's your business doing?"

"Last year the store met expenses and this year I was going to show a profit until I had to come here in December and add three thousand dollars to inventory."

Betsy said, "Don't open the bags."

"Huh?"

She explained the ploy of storing the purchases unopened until after the first of the new year.

Harry nodded, smiling. "I guess I'll be in the black after all. Thank you."

"I'm Lenore King, and I love those Professor Fizzby patterns of yours, Mr. Nolan," said a tall, very slender woman of perhaps forty summers. She wore a loose-fitting blue chambray shirt that matched her eyes, and her dark brown hair was pulled back and fastened with a scrunchie at the nape of her neck. Her lips were smiling, but not her eyes.

"Thanks," said Terrance carelessly.

"Give her praise its due," said Betsy, "this is the designer of that sampler Christmas tree Bewitching Stitches is selling."

Terrence looked at her with more respect. "I saw that," he said. "Someone told me about it and I went for a look. Samplers aren't my thing, but that is downright ingenious."

She blushed and crumbled the fragment of dinner roll into crumbs with her long fingers.

"You're very kind," she muttered. "Especially since the model is such a mess."

Godwin said, "What suite is Bewitching Stitches in? I'd like to take a look at it."

Betsy said, "Suite five seventeen. Go look if you like, but I've already bought four copies of the pattern." She smiled and added, "I made a note to warn my customers that it needs careful, professional finishing."

Lenore's blush deepened, and she pinched the last crumbs between her fingers so hard her fingernails turned white. She said, "Don't bother. The model's probably been thrown away. I spilled coffee all over it awhile ago."

"Oh, too bad!" said Godwin.

"It's all right, it wasn't exactly a showpiece. I didn't get my good model in time for Nashville. I had to bring the working piece, all crooked and full of loose threads. It's affecting sales, and I'm afraid Bewitching Stitches isn't going to buy any more of my work."

"A lot of people were caught on the hop when the Market got pushed back to December," Terrence said.

Lenore hesitated, frowning, then made up her mind and said, "The thing is, I had it stitched in plenty of time. This was important—it's my first pattern for Bewitching Stitches. But the store where I took it for finishing messed me up. They know me there, they knew it was a debut for the Nashville Market, we talked about it. Belle wrote down that I needed it by February 10. When they changed the date to December, I came in and told them, but she didn't call the finisher to change the due date."

Betsy said in a low, horrified voice, "How could they do something so irresponsible?" It was bad enough not to get a piece finished in time for a birth or Christmas or a wedding, but you could always give the present after the date. There was no way to retro-present a new model; this offense was magnitudes greater.

"Are you sure they knew about the change in date?" she asked.

"Of course I'm sure!" said Lenore. "The owners were coming to the Market. They knew the piece was supposed to be shown here. How could they not know? I told Cherry and I saw her write the note to Belle."

"That's *terrible*!" agreed Godwin.

Lenore nodded. "I was furious, of course. But I didn't kill her."

Godwin laughed once, "Ha!" then added uncertainly, "Well, good for you."

"Who didn't you kill?" Jill asked. Her voice was very quiet.

"Belle Hammermill, of course." Lenore's eyes were firmly fixed on her plate. "She's the one who's dead, isn't she? I think she messed me up on purpose, for some sick reason of her own. I wished she would die." Her eyes suddenly lifted and went around the table, taking in their amazed stares. "That's right, I even told people I wished she would take poison and die. And now she's over there on the floor, dead, and I can't be pleased. I just feel sick and scared. Is that stupid, or what?"

There was a hasty chorus of disagreement, and Betsy said, "It's not stupid. You wish her dead, and she dies—that's scary. But wishing doesn't make it so. Think how many times you've wished for something that doesn't happen. This was a coincidence. And what happened to Belle was an accident, we all know that."

Lenore took a breath as if to reply, gave a little hiccup as if changing her mind hastily, and said instead, "You're right, I guess."

"Did you ever think Ms. Hammermill was very unhappy or even seriously depressed?" Jill asked.

"What do you mean?" Betsy said. "You think she committed suicide?" The image of Belle going over the railing rose up in Betsy's mind. "It didn't look like suicide to me."

Lenore, looking into her lap again said, "Of course it wasn't suicide. Belle wouldn't do something like that. She was enjoying herself, she always enjoyed herself. Whenever any unhappiness came around, she laid it right away on someone else." She blinked rapidly and her chin began to tremble. "Excuse me," she said and pushed her chair back so hard its metal legs shrieked on the tile floor.

The men stood, Terrence reaching as if to take her hand, his eyes concerned. But it was Jill who got to her first, taking her shoulders in a firm grip.

"Is there someone here with you? A friend?"

"N-no, not really. Mr. Moore, he owns Bewitching Stitches, he's my sponsor. I'm supposed to be up there talking to his customers, but I can't go back there. I think I'll just go up to my room."

"No," said Jill firmly. "Go back to Bewitching Stitches. You saw how people here liked your pattern. Others will too, and will want to talk to you about it. I'll stop by in half an hour to see how you're getting along. If you still want to get away, I'll take you back to my suite."

"But—" Lenore gestured up and around, taking in the Market and its purpose.

"It's all right. You see, I'm not a shop-owner; I'm supposed to be at another hotel, at another event. Betsy Devonshire and Godwin DuLac are old friends, I took them to dinner at my hotel last night and when I brought them back here, I couldn't leave because of the snow. So I'm sitting up all alone in their suite stitching. I wouldn't mind sharing the time with someone else."

Lenore had stiffened in Jill's grip, and looked away from the curious faces at the table. But Jill turned her so they could look into one another's eyes. There is something about being held firmly by the shoulders while being smiled at by a wise and sympathetic face.

Lenore relaxed a bit and grudged, "Okay. Yes. See you later."

Jill released her and she turned and walked away. Jill sat down again and turned to Betsy.

"Now, just what did you mean when you said it didn't look like suicide to you?"

Eleven

"Say, who died and left you the chief of police?" demanded Harry Mason, with a grin.

Jill looked around the table and saw Terrence frowning at her, too. At first she said nothing, absorbing the indignant curiosity effortlessly. Then she sighed and relented. "I'm not a chief of police, I'm Sergeant Jill Cross Larson, a desk sergeant with a very small police department in Minnesota." She took up her fork to attack her salad.

"See, I knew she was a cop," nodded Harry, but he was as surprised as he was pleased at being right.

"So what are you doing here in Nashville?" asked Terrence.

"I'm in town for an administration seminar."

"You mean there's another event here at the Consulate besides the Market?" Harry was amazed.

"No, it's at the Grand Ole Opry Hotel. I gave Betsy and Godwin a ride back to this hotel last night and the weather was too bad to get away again. Then this happened, and when I found out the local gendarmes couldn't get here right away, I decided to take a little action." She shrugged. "You wear a badge long enough, and you tend to take action in situations like this." She looked at Betsy. "So tell me how come you're so sure this was an accident?"

Betsy said, "Because I saw it happen."

Godwin dropped his fork and said, *"Strewth!"*

Betsy said, "What? What's the matter?"

"I thought it was terrible that I was sitting down here when she fell!" Godwin said. "Do you mean you actually *saw* her go over?"

"Yes, I did. But there were hundreds of people walking around when it happened, I'm sure I'm not the only one." She looked around the table, and said, more faintly, "Am I?"

"I've only talked to one other eyewitness, and she didn't see her actually go over," Jill said.

Betsy's frown deepened. "I can't believe I'm the only one!"

"Where were you when you saw her?" asked Jill.

"Well, let's see. I'd just come out of BritStitch, which is on five, on the west side."

"What did you see?" asked Jill.

Betsy paused, for two reasons. She didn't want to talk about it—and she wanted to get it right. "Okay, I came out and there were some people talking and I joined them for a minute. They went away and I would have, too, but I just happened to look up and saw this woman standing there. She was leaning on the rail and her hand slipped." Betsy gulped at the memory, then continued, "She just kind of fell forward, and once her shoulder went over, she just kept going, right over and down."

Godwin shuddered and Terrence closed his eyes. "God bless us, every one," said Harry, and it wasn't a joke.

Jill asked in her calm voice, "Did you see anyone else up there with her?"

"No. And I'm sure about that. She was standing all alone up there, I was kind of struck by that. I didn't want to see her, er, land, so I kept my eyes on where she fell from, and there was no one else there, the railing was empty."

"That's interesting," said Jill.

"Why, did your other eyewitness see someone?"

"No, she also said she saw Ms. Hammermill standing alone at the railing immediately before the accident. But she didn't see Ms. Hammermill actually go over."

"So what's the matter?" asked Godwin. "Betsy is saying the same thing your witness is."

"The matter is, I can't understand how someone could accidentally fall over one of those railings." She lifted one shoulder in half a shrug. "Suicide is a possible explanation, of course." She speared a grape tomato with her fork.

But Betsy frowned. "What I saw didn't seem like suicide. I still think it was an accident."

Harry said, "I know of another witness. I was talking with Dave Stott—he's Norden Crafts, of course—and he said he was in the Kreinik suite when it happened. He said Doug Kreinik was looking out the door when she, er, went by. And Dave looked up right after she went over and there was no one up where she'd been standing. He said he had a good, clear view from outside the Kreinik suite."

"What number is Kreinik's suite?" asked Jill.

"I'm not sure . . ."

Godwin reached into a pocket. "Just a second." He pulled out a folded copy of the Market listing. He turned to the section listing suppliers alphabetically and said, "Six twenty-five." And, before anyone could ask, paged back and said, "BritStitch is in five seventeen."

"Opposite sides," confirmed Terrence, nodding.

"Thank you," nodded Jill.

Betsy said, "So see? Now three people agree that no one was up there with Belle before she fell. Now will you drop that idea that there's something funny about this?"

"I'm assuming nothing, yet," Jill said. "But a hand slips and a person goes over? Maybe, if he's a drunk, and also if he's a basketball star so the railing hits him below his bend-over point."

Betsy looked up. Those railings didn't look all that high to her.

Jill continued, "But if she was all alone, then maybe it was a suicide. Did anyone here at this table know her? Besides Lenore, I mean."

The others all shook their heads.

Then Godwin said, "I didn't talk to Belle, but she had a partner in her shop who I talked to. Her name's Cherry Pye—for real, isn't that cute? She uses a wheelchair."

"You talked to her after Belle died, and down here, on this floor, right?" asked Betsy.

"Yes, how did you know?"

"I saw you—or I thought it was you—talking to a woman in a wheelchair. This was right after it happened. She seemed to be crying."

"Yes, that's right," nodded Godwin. "I saw her at one of

these tables, crying and looking awful, and so I came to see if I could help. She said she was Belle Hammermill's partner in business, a shop in Milwaukee. She asked me to stay with her until she got her courage back and she could go do what needed to be done. So I did."

"Did she say anything about Belle?" asked Jill.

"She said—" He paused to think about it. "I was like you, wondering if maybe it was a suicide, so I asked her if Belle was depressed or upset over anything. She said no."

"Did she say anything else?"

This was sounding more and more like an interrogation, and Betsy was feeling more and more uncomfortable. *Not here, not here,* she thought. It was bad enough to be mixed up in murders at home, but it was awful to think she brought the contagion with her on her travels.

Godwin was saying, "Ms. Pye said she was more forgetful lately, and Cherry wondered if she had something on her mind."

"Something on her mind?" Terrence said. "If it was suicide, surely it would stick out a mile!"

Betsy said, reluctantly, "I talked with someone else who knew her."

Jill asked, "Who was it?"

"Her name is Eve Suttle, or Saddle. She used to work for Belle, but now works for another shop in Savannah. I was coming out of our suite when I saw her. She was actually sitting on the floor, crying. So I walked her down to her room."

"Is her room near ours?" asked Jill.

"No. As a matter of fact, it's down a floor, on seven."

"So what was she doing on eight?"

"She did one of those mental blank things, thinking about

something else while riding the elevator, and just rode it right past her floor."

"Did she say anything about Belle?"

"She said Belle helped her get her life together." Betsy frowned, remembering her final remark. "But I got the impression she either quit in anger or was fired. She went home to Savannah, she said, though she didn't have an accent. She has a little girl," Betsy concluded irrelevantly.

She saw something in Jill's eyes and said, "Now wait, I met Eve on eight, and Belle fell from the ninth floor." Involuntarily, her eyes went up to look at the top gallery, high over the dais in front of the lobby, and everyone's else's head swiveled upward as well.

"Long way down from there," murmured Harry.

Terrence shuddered. "Oh, please, hush!" he said. "Now I'm going to have to walk close to the walls and all I'll be able to think about is tripping and going over. Brrr, it gives me chills! Honestly, why this has to happen at Market, and mess up everyone's head, I don't know! It's going to be like a funeral in here the rest of the weekend!"

"I wish they'd come and take the body away," said Harry. He looked at Jill. "Can't the hotel at least move it out of here? Put it in a back room or something?"

"No," said Jill. "I've instructed them to leave the body where it is until the police arrive. Or until we know for sure it was an accident."

Betsy said, "Maybe she was looking down, and you know how it is when you look down from the top of a high place, like you want to jump."

Terrence said, "I'm like that. I can't stand high places, they make my fingers and toes tingle and I get dizzy and start leaning forward, more and than more . . ." He shook his hands hard to rid them of the tingling. "Ugh!"

Harry said, "Since my accident, I can't even look out a second-story window."

Godwin, pleased to be the brave one, said, "I adore high places. The Eiffel Tower is one of my favorites."

Terrence said, "Now, that's different; looking out from high, *romantic* places isn't scary! Especially when . . ." He let that thought drift unfinished over their heads, while he flashed his dimple at Godwin, who batted his eyelashes and actually managed a blush.

Betsy heaved a big sigh. Godwin's partner at home was the jealous type, but she was secretly grateful the subject was changing. Godwin looked at her, reading her mind, and grinned most mischievously.

"I wonder if she'll try to keep the shop going," said Harry.

"Who?" asked Godwin.

"This partner, Cherry Pye," Harry said. "I suppose she might, if she could find another partner. A person in a wheelchair couldn't manage by herself, could she?"

"It's way too early for that kind of decision," said Betsy, remembering how long it was after her sister's death before she knew she would keep Crewel World open.

"Partnerships can get tricky when one partner leaves," noted Terrence. "Especially when it's the way this one did. Unexpectedly, I mean."

Godwin said, "Maybe the partnership was in the early stages of breaking up anyway. I think she said something . . ." He thought a moment, then shook his head, unable to remember whatever it was.

Terrance said, "Well, remember Lenore at this very table,

all upset because she was so angry at Belle she wished her dead—and now she is."

Jill said quietly, "So that makes two, maybe, who wanted Belle to die."

Betsy said, "I wonder . . . That woman, Eve Saddle—Sutter?—whatever her name is, who used to work for Belle. Something about the way she talked about quitting her job with Belle . . ."

"Three, then," Jill said. "Maybe there are others."

Harry said, "It *stinks* to have people wishing you dead!"

Godwin said, "Now, Jill, don't go thinking what I think you're thinking. We have eyewitnesses to tell us she wasn't thrown over that railing."

Betsy seconded that extra-heartily. "That's right!"

Jill said, "Eyewitnesses are wrong fairly often."

Harry said, "I wonder if this Cherry Pye is going to sue the hotel? You know, loss of the business because the partner died. And she died because the railings are too low, or because there are no nets to catch people who fall over them."

"Oh, come on!" scoffed Terrence.

But Harry insisted, "If my folks gave me a joke name like that, I'd be cranky all my life. And cranky people sue."

Twelve

Saturday, 1:45 P.M.

After lunch, Jill went up to Bewitching Stitches. She paused in the doorway and saw Lenore talking earnestly with a customer. Lenore had two fingers of one hand supporting an arm of her model, and stained and sagging as it was, the gesture was of a new mother showing off her baby. The customer had her head cocked doubtfully. Lenore picked up a sheet of her pattern and explained something. The customer took it, and Lenore tipped her model and gestured at a lower quarter of it.

Another customer paused to look at Lenore and listen to her talk. The first customer shook her head, put the pattern sheet down, and backed away, but the second stooped for a closer look. Lenore shifted her attention to the second customer, who was both frowning and nodding. Jill nodded too, and went away. Lenore might still be having a hard time making a sale with only that sorry model to help, but at least she was back in there trying.

Back up in Betsy's suite, Jill sat down with her needlework. But she didn't get past picking up her needle. She sat with it in her fingers, the Connie Welch Santa head on her lap, neither of them with any hold on her attention.

Suppose Belle's death was not an accident? Suppose Lenore was a murderer? Which would be the more clever way to behave? To continue trying to sell her work, or to allow shock to dictate a retreat to the privacy of her room?

But it wouldn't be a private retreat, would it? Jill had offered to sit with her, and that would mean questions to answer, a posture to maintain, under close scrutiny. If Lenore was guilty, she would absolutely choose to avoid that.

Of course, even if she had nothing to do with Belle's death, it might still be better to continue to do what she came here to do, help sell her new pattern.

So maybe deciding to remain on duty at Bewitching Stitches was perfectly innocent, and in fact a wise thing to do. Which still didn't mean Belle's death was an accident.

True, the cream of the law-abiding middle class was gathered here, businessmen and businesswomen engaged in buying and selling materials related to that most decorous of crafts—stitchery. Such people did not normally toss one another over ninth-story railings. When she was offered an eyewitness who said she saw the woman go over after standing by the railing alone, it would have been entirely understandable to think it was an accident. The possibility of error was like a feather weighed against the outsize bucket of wet sand that was a policeman's normal workload.

Come to it, why *did* she wonder if it might be murder?

Because despite Betsy's account, an accident seemed unlikely. The people who built this hotel were not stupid. They wouldn't install such low railings that a slipping hand would let someone go over. Jill glanced toward the open door of the suite, at the railing. It appeared to be at least forty inches high, so unless one were seven feet tall, the top of the railing struck anybody who blundered into it well above the hips. And Belle Hammermill was about five feet four. And last seen *standing* at the railing, not running into it. As for that curious tendency in some humans to gaze down from heights until they fell, surely the flower boxes hanging on the outside of the rail prevented one from looking straight down and inducing that kind of hypnosis.

How about suicide then? People who committed suicide by jumping from a height in a public place tended to stand on the edge for a considerable while, some to gather the nerve, others to gather a crowd. While Belle had stood there long enough for at least two people to notice, apparently she hadn't stood there very long, or there would have been more witnesses coming forward to say, "I saw her standing there," or, "I saw her fall."

Wait a minute. There might be more witnesses. Someone—Jill, perhaps—should go around and ask.

She reached for the name tag that gave her permission to wander the sales floors and set out for the lobby. No need to rush down the stairs this time, so she headed for the elevators.

There were four elevators, two each in the center of the long sides of the atrium. They were made of thick panes of beveled glass set in polished brass frames that came to pointed tops, which gave them a spurious Victorian style. While not made giddy by watching the floor rush up as the elevator went down, Jill nevertheless kept her eyes on the upper floors, and noted how quickly people vanished behind the flower boxes as the elevator descended.

She went out to the front desk. Marveen, looking very tired now, managed a faint smile as Jill came up to the counter. "Sergeant Larson," she said with a nod.

"Ms. Harrison," replied Jill. "No relief for you yet?" She looked out the big front windows and saw the snowfall had at least paused, though the sky remained overcast.

"Oh, no, the city's still at a complete standstill."

"That's too bad."

"You don't know the half of it," sighed Marveen.

Jill, feeling a little chill, cocked her head sideways in a show of sympathy. "Like what?" she asked.

"Well, for one thing, no delivery trucks. We're out of fresh produce for the kitchen, and our supplies of milk and meat are very low, because we've got a full house. In fact, more than full; we've had to double up in a few rooms because some guests who were supposed to leave Friday morning are still here and will still be here on Sunday if we don't get a thaw started soon. And I even have some people bunking down in the conference rooms."

Jill nearly smiled, because none of the problems were of a criminal nature. "That's serious, but none of your troubles are visible to the guests, so you're doing a good job of handling it. Of course, I hadn't thought about food deliveries; that might start showing soon."

Marveen nodded emphatically. "Like in the morning. No fresh bread for toast."

"Is your chef good at improvising?"

Marveen laughed softly. "He says he is. I have a feeling we're going to find out."

Jill smiled back, then sobered. "I was wondering if you could give me some information about some of your guests."

"Well, it depends on what you want to know. Or is this like police business?"

"It is. Of course, if I find out anything significant, all I can do is hand it along to the local investigator. But at least I can help carry the load right here."

Marveen nodded; she would not have shared her troubles if she didn't consider Jill an official rather than a guest. "Can you do this without aggravating our guests?"

"I'll sure try."

Marveen sighed at that weak promise. "What do you want to know?"

"Can you tell me what room Ms. Cherry Pye is in? I assume she shared a room with Belle Hammermill."

"Well, she didn't, actually," said Marveen. "Ms. Pye needs a suite specially equipped for the handicapped. It has special features, like a no-threshold shower and extra-wide doorways. Ms. Hammermill failed to mention that when she made a reservation for herself and Ms. Pye, but fortunately we had a suite available suited to her special needs when Ms. Pye contacted us to confirm the reservation. She elected to have the handicapped suite to herself."

Jill nodded at this hint of a rift between Cherry and Belle. "Is this the first time Ms. Hammermill and Ms. Pye have come to the Nashville Market?"

"I have no idea. I know there are generally several people in wheelchairs at these events, but I don't know if we keep records of guests from year to year. Molly is our bookkeeper, but of course she's not here today."

"No, of course not."

It turned out Cherry's suite was on nine, a few doors down from Belle Hammermill's. Jill wrote that down and found that Lenore King was also on nine and there was no Eve Saddle. There was an Eve, but her name was Suttle—"That must be it, Betsy wasn't sure of the name," said Jill—and her suite was on seven. She wrote down the room numbers and thanked Marveen.

Jill turned away from the desk toward the clusters of up-holstered chairs and comfortable sofas, where several groups of women sat stitching. She went to each group and then to the INRG committee members behind the long tables, asking casual questions about what they were working on or how the event was going, and then mentioning as if in passing that she wondered if anyone had actually seen Belle Hammermill fall. Or if they knew of anyone else who might have seen something.

When anyone asked why—and someone always did—she said she was a police officer from a different jurisdiction assisting the locals, who were tied up with weather-related emergencies.

"This was probably an accident," said Jill, but she was collecting any details while everyone's memories were still fresh. "This will help them clear their records," Jill said, her casual tone making it not important.

She went back to Betsy's suite and dialed Betsy's cell phone. "Can you talk?" Jill asked.

"Wait a minute." It only took a few seconds before Betsy said, "What's up?"

"I want to find out how many people here might have had a reason to murder Belle."

There was a surprised silence. Then, "You *still* think this was murder?"

"I'm curious about her death. Where are you right now?"

"I'm outside Rainbow Gallery, in one of the side hallways next to the stairs."

"Walk back up to the atrium, right up to the railing."

"All right." There was another pause, which gradually filled with the sound of people talking in a great empty space. "Okay," said Betsy. "Now what?"

"How high is the railing on you?"

"Oh, it's . . ." Yet another pause. "It's up past the bottom of my rib cage. Almost to the bra line, actually. I didn't realize that. But hey, I'm *short*, Jill."

"Belle was about your height. Stretch your hand out over the railing, like you're waving to someone."

There was a suppressed giggle. "Is this another one of your stupid pranks?" On rare occasions Jill displayed a penchant for practical jokes.

"No."

"Well, okay then. Hi, there!"

"Now, reach farther, put your shoulder out there, reaching for a helium balloon that's escaped."

"Uff. Okay, I'm out there. Durn, I missed it. Jill, people are looking."

"Smile at them."

"Okay, smiling."

"Now, try to lean out, follow your shoulder out over the railing."

"Can't—uff—can't do it. Why—? Oh. . ."

"I didn't think so."

"Well, all right. But I saw her, Jill. She didn't, you know, throw a leg over. Not that it would be easy for someone as short as me to do that. Funny how this railing doesn't look all that high, until you're right up against it."

"So if she didn't slip, and she didn't climb up to jump," prompted Jill.

"No," said Betsy. "I don't believe it, I *won't* believe it."

"I take it that means you don't want to come along while I talk to people."

"Absolutely not."

"Okay."

"But Jill?" That came just in time to stop Jill signing off. "Yes?"

"Let me know what they say, all right?"

"Sure."

Thirteen

Through the door to the lobby came a tall man, about forty-five, dark-haired and slope-shouldered, with a big, hard belly and bad feet that distorted his unshined black oxfords. His shoes made squishing sounds—Marveen heard the noise and that's what drew her attention around—and the bottoms of his trousers were wet, the left leg up to the knee in front, indicating a half-fall. He was unbuttoning his raincoat, which was damp about the shoulders from the snow melting on it. He needed a shave and his small, dark eyes were red-rimmed. But there was a dogged air about him, as if he was a man used to being exhausted.

He paused a few moments just inside the door to the lobby, perhaps to listen to trombones crooning "White Christmas," more likely to simply breathe air that was not clogged with snow, and stand secure on a level surface not coated with ice.

Marveen wondered how he had managed to climb the hill—he hadn't come up in a vehicle, the portico outside the doors was empty. And why had he come alone? Didn't the police generally travel in pairs? This man was, she knew, a policeman. For one thing he looked like one; for another, no one else would make the effort it must have taken to get here. He came to the desk and, reaching into an inside pocket, said, "I'm Lieutenant Paul Birdsong, Nashville PD. Someone here called about a fatal accident?"

"That would be me," said Marveen. "I'm Marveen Harrison, acting hotel manager." She was very good at reading people's needs, and he needed his questions answered briefly and directly. They both spoke quietly, because the chairs and couches in the lobby held nine women who had been talking and stitching until he came in, when a nosy silence had fallen.

"Have you moved the body?" he asked, replacing the wallet that held his badge and ID card.

"No, we thought we should leave her just as she is."

"That's good. Where is she?"

"Out here in the atrium, behind those screens. Do you want to look right away?"

He did. He went heavily down the steps and pulled one screen open like a door. It moved easily, if noisily, on the tile floor. He stood completely still for nearly a minute, just looking.

Marveen wondered what conclusions he was drawing as

she struggled against the urge to look, too, to try to see it through his eyes. But what he was looking at was something no longer fresh, something settled into death, a horrible *thing* that used to be a living guest of the hotel, and now something no one wants to look at. Marveen looked instead at the dark-haired woman in a green pantsuit seated on a folding chair on the other side of the screens. Marveen didn't know who she was; she was younger than the woman in red who had first sat there, and the woman in black who had replaced her. Marveen nodded at her to let her know that the man who had opened the screen had the authority to do so. The woman had already concluded that—Birdsong did not look merely curious—and she just nodded back.

Marveen continued to avoid seeing the body by next checking to see that the two white cockatoos in their cage had been tended to, and noting that the bottom of the little pool of water beside them was strewn with far fewer coins than usual. Possibly the hardheaded shop-owners and wholesalers weren't the kind to throw money away. Or, more likely, they didn't want to approach the screens.

"Terrible." Marveen looked up. Birdsong was shaking his head as he stepped back and slid the screen back into place. "I hate looking at jumpers," he remarked.

"I understand," she said.

"You've identified her," he said, and it was not quite a question.

"Yes, she's Ms. Belle Hammermill, here for the needle-work market. She's from Milwaukee where she owned a store called Belle's Samplers and More. She had a partner in the business, a woman named Cherry Pye—" Birdsong snorted faintly. "Yes, I know, but that's her real name. Ms. Pye identified the body."

Birdsong had pulled a fat little notebook from a pocket. "When did Ms. Hammermill die?" he asked.

"About ten-twenty this morning. I was behind the counter in the lobby and heard her scream as she fell."

"Do you know what floor she fell from?"

"Yes, the ninth floor directly over us." Birdsong looked up, and so did Marveen. With their flower boxes and trailing ivy, the railings made a soft, attractive, repeating pattern up to a skylit roof far overhead. There were perhaps a dozen curious faces peering down at them from various floors. Most of them hastily withdrew on seeing their looks returned.

"She went over the top railing?" he asked, squinting a little and moving back a few steps for a better look.

"Yes."

"Do you know how it happened?"

"Yes, it was an accident. We have an eyewitness."

Birdsong's head came down quickly as hope dawned in his eyes. "An actual eyewitness?"

"Yes, she saw Ms. Hammermill standing by the railing and then go over. She says she was all alone up there."

"What's her name, this eyewitness?"

"Samantha Wills. She's also a guest at the hotel, here for the market."

"Market?"

"Virtually all our guests here right now are either buying or selling needlework patterns and materials. It's an annual event, this is its fourteenth year." She frowned. "Well, actually, it's still the thirteenth. Usually it's held in February, but we had to move it back two months. A booking problem."

"How do I get to talk to Samantha Wills?"

"She has a cell phone and I have the number."

"Will you call her for me?"

"Certainly. Would you like to wait in the office? It's quiet and private. And you can sit down."

"Thank you."

Marveen started back for the lobby. "It will probably take a few minutes for her to get down here. Would you like a cup of coffee?"

"Yes. Yes, I would." Birdsong ran a thick hand over his face, his fingers making a sound on his unshaven jowls.

"Would it be presumptuous of me to offer you something to eat? I think we have sweet rolls left from breakfast. Or I could order a sandwich."

Another hope-filled smile formed, sweeter even than the response to the news that this was a witnessed accident. "A sandwich, yes. Would you mind?"

"I don't know what kind it will be; we haven't had any deliveries since yesterday noon."

"Whatever you can scrounge up, and I thank you. No onion or lettuce or tomato, okay? And I like my coffee black."

"I'll have it brought on a tray to the office."

"Thank you."

Marveen showed him the entrance through the counter and into the back office, which was large and decidedly chilly. Snow was again whirling thickly past the two tall windows. There were two desks in the room, and six filing cabinets. The larger desk was clear of everything but a big blotter and a phone. The chair behind it was black leather. Birdsong sank into it with a sound that was more a groan than a sigh.

"Oh, by the way," said Marveen, and his eyes closed in pain before he looked at her, braced for bad news. "There's a police officer from Minnesota who had already talked to Ms. Wills. Would you like to talk to her, as well?"

"Oh, yes, by all means."

Marveen couldn't tell if he was being sarcastic or not, so she only nodded and withdrew to make her phone calls.

Samantha Wills came trotting into the lobby sixteen minutes later, still in her stretch pants. "Sorry I took so long, I was loaded down with things and thought, egh-hem, I should take them to my room first." The anxious look was back, and she cleared her throat again as she waited for Marveen to let Sergeant Birdsong know she was here. Marveen opened the door and noted that the plate on which a roast beef sandwich, a generous fistful of potato chips, and a long pickle slice had rested nine minutes earlier had not even any crumbs left on it as a reminder of the meal. Birdsong was bent over his coffee cup as if drawing warmth from it up his nose. His eyes were closed.

"Uh," she said, and he started and looked around at her. "Ms. Wills is here."

"Fine, send her in." He stood slowly, and Marveen stepped back to wave in the obese woman. She was still clearing her throat and her fingers were touching her neck as she went. Marveen closed the door and went to call Sergeant Larson.

The Minnesota police officer came into the lobby a few minutes later. Marveen invited her to sit behind the counter, out of the way of the stitchers.

While they waited, the big front doors swooped open and two young men in white trousers, knit watch caps, heavy black pea coats and black rubber boots came in. They carried a wire stretcher with a blue plastic lining between them.

They stood a few moments inside the door, stamping snow off their boots. The stitchers stopped working to stare, their faces showing concern. Marveen raised her hand, and they came to the counter. "There is a police investigator inside the office," she said, gesturing at the door to it. "I'll tell him you're here."

"Thanks," said the younger of the two.

Marveen rapped once and opened the door. Ms. Wills was sitting at the side of the bigger desk in the office chair that belonged to the other desk. She no longer looked nervous; in fact, she was smiling just a little. Investigator Birdsong rose in Marveen's opinion from competent to *good*.

"Yes?" said Birdsong impatiently.

"Emergency services is here."

"Wonderful. Excuse me, Ms. Wills." Birdsong came out and held a brief conversation with the young men and then waved them and their stretcher into the atrium.

With a minimum of noise and fuss, they put the unfortunate Ms. Hammermill into the stretcher—the blue lining turned out to be a body bag—carried her through the lobby. The stitchers all stood as she went by, and two went to hold the big double doors open.

Saturday, 3:40 P.M.

Jill waited patiently behind the check-in counter for Investigator Birdsong to ask for her. She watched the ambulance crew arrive, consult with Birdsong, and take away the body of Belle Hammermill.

It was always a solemn moment, to watch someone being carried away in a body bag. There was no rush to it, as there was when the person's face was showing. Several of the people sitting on the lobby couches stood as the stretcher went by, and a man and woman hurried to hold the doors open.

Jill stood, too, and took a moment to wish Belle's soul good fortune in the sudden new place it had found itself.

Then she sat down again, thoughtful. So long as a body remained where it had fallen, Jill was able to think of it primarily as a problem and/or a source of information. Once it was gone, she was generally able to stop thinking about it. But during that minute or two of transition, while it was being taken away, it became a human tragedy. And though Jill rarely discussed philosophical questions out loud, her work was the kind that raised them. Was there something after death? Was it golden gates and angels singing? Was there, at least, an explanation for everything? Or was death the final blank, and dying much as described in poet Philip Larkin's vision of a black ship coming into port for you, towing behind it "a huge and birdless silence"?

Though a Christian, Jill wasn't absolutely sure it wasn't the last—but, as she reflected at every death she attended, *the deceased now knew.* And just in case, Jill recited a very old prayer against the darkness, "May perpetual light shine upon her."

So long as she was in a prayer mode, she wished the two medics and all emergency workers, strength and patience. It was going to be a very long shift.

She sat down again to wait.

A few minutes later, Birdsong came to the door to show Samantha Wills out and her in. Samantha looked heartened, no longer the frightened, nervous woman Jill had interviewed that morning.

"Come in, sit down," Birdsong said to Jill, in a voice roughened by exhaustion.

She obeyed.

"The hotel lady says you're a cop from Minnesota. That right?" he asked, as he turned away and she followed him. The room was delightfully cool.

"Yes, sir." She produced identification, and explained how she happened to be at the Consulate instead of the Grand Ole Opry Hotel.

He looked over the badge and ID card, raising his eyes once to compare the photo to her actual face. "You're missing some good parties over there," he noted.

"And not having one here," she replied.

"Yeah, this's too bad. What do you think?"

"There are at least three people here who were very unhappy with Belle Hammermill. But there's another eyewitness besides Samantha, someone I know personally as reliable, who says she watched it happen. She says Belle was alone up there. She says it seemed to her that Ms. Hammermill's hand slipped and she fell forward and over. I have another eyewitness account, this one third hand, that says a Mr. Dave Stott looked up right after she fell and the railing was empty."

"Yeah. This partner she had—" He consulted his notes. "—Cherry Pye." He shook his head at the foolishness of some parents in naming their children. "You talk to her?"

"No, but someone else I know did, and he says Ms. Pye said Belle wasn't suicidal. Ms. Pye, by the way, is one of the people very upset with Belle. I did talk to someone else who frequented Belle and Cherry's shop and who had an infuriating experience with them just before this event. She didn't think Belle was suicidal, either."

"So," he said, "two who knew her say she wasn't inclined to jump. And while you got three people mad at her, two, maybe three, saw her all alone up there, and not being pushed. And what you got at this hotel is just these low railings to stand between crowds of people and a big empty space. That adds up to an accident, right?" He wrote that conclusion down in his notebook and stood. Then he noticed she hadn't risen and said, "What?"

"The railings are three and a half feet high, which isn't low at all. And where she was, wasn't crowded. And she wasn't so tall that leaning out would overbalance her."

"So?"

"Well," she persisted, "I'd at least like to find another witness who actually saw her fall over."

"So would I. If this were an ordinary day, I'd do that. I might even bring a crew in here. But nine times out of ten, what would I find out? Just what I already got—an accident. She was standing up there all alone, she saw someone a couple floors down and tried to get her attention and fell. Or she had a secret sorrow and here was a chance to end her troubles. Or she's like a couple other cases I've heard of where she looked over and saw how high up she was and gave in to that weird impulse to jump."

Jill, a person subject to authority, nodded. "It could very well be one of those."

"Sure." He closed the notebook with a little flip of his hand and put his ballpoint pen back into his shirt pocket. "I wish they were all this easy. I've been up since yesterday morning, and I got six more places to get to before I can go home to shower and change clothes and come right back to work. The National Guard volunteered us a couple of Hummers and I got one, otherwise I'd be home watching the Weather Channel like everyone else in Nashville today. You want a ride back to the Grand Ole Opry Hotel?"

Jill shook her head. "I'm going to stay. If I hear anything, should I contact you?"

He looked at her out of his reddened eyes, breathing audibly while he thought about that. His expression did not change when he started to fumble in an inside coat pocket, or when he brought out a business card.

"Sure, why not?" he said, and gave the card to her. Then he turned and led the way out of the office.

Fourteen

Saturday, 3:55 P.M.

Betsy went into the last suite on this long side of the third floor, a suite less crowded with product than most. STARDUST, the sign read. She was immediately struck by a large depiction of an old-fashioned steam locomotive. It was a snowy winter scene; the locomotive had pulled into a village decorated for Christmas, with wreaths on every door. The locomotive itself had a wreath circling its single head-light and a red ribbon streaming from its bell. Adults in fur-collared coats and children in snowsuits were waving at the engineer, who was waving back. The locomotive was pulling two yellow passenger cars and a red caboose—it was sad to think that modern children didn't know what a caboose was.

But that's not why Betsy was disappointed. "Oh," she said, "I thought that was a cross-stitch pattern."

"But it is," replied a young woman with shining brown hair and hazel eyes, gesturing to a rack. "Come over here to see it. I begin all my patterns as paintings."

"Oh? Oh, good!" Betsy went smiling to the rack and picked up a pattern of the railroad engine. *Phil*, she was thinking. Phil Galvin was a retired railroad engineer, a semi-regular in the group that gathered on Monday afternoons in Betsy's shop to stitch and gossip. His favorite patterns reflected his interest in trains. Because he also had a fondness for Christmas, this was a sure sale. She bought a second one, because someone would see Phil working on it and want to know where to get one, and then a third, because there was also a happy little group of historical restoration people in the Twin Cities that specialized in old steam locomotives. And she took a business card, in case there were more requests for the pattern.

The brown-haired woman said, "I'm Linda Kotilla, and I painted these pictures." She smiled to see Betsy taking other patterns of her design from the racks. "I'm glad to see you like my work. I use my little hometown as a model."

Sure enough, Betsy could see that the buildings in other charts were the same as in the painting, small and built of cream-colored wood, just from different angles. "Oh, they're all beautiful, though of course I can't stitch anything so complex myself. But I know my customers, and there are some who will just love them."

Betsy paid for the patterns, then went out to the elevator. She was about to get on when she heard a familiar voice call her name, and looked around. It sounded like Godwin, but she couldn't see him. Then he called a third time and she looked out and up, and there he was, four stories up and around the side, waving at her from the railing. Betsy waved back.

"Jill wants you to come on up," he called.

"To the suite?" she called back.

"No, here," said Jill, suddenly appearing beside Godwin.

"All right!" The elevator doors had closed by then, but that was fine, because it was headed down.

"What is it, what's up?" asked Betsy a few minutes later, getting out on seven and finding the two waiting for her at the elevator.

"Did you see me with Godwin?" asked Jill.

"Sure," said Betsy.

"I mean when you first looked up and saw him waving at you," persisted Jill.

"Well, no. You came up beside him after he called to get my attention."

"She's the one who pointed you out and told me to call to you," said Godwin. "She was standing right behind me."

"No, that's impossible, Goddy," said Betsy. "I was looking right at you, and you were up there alone." Jill was at least two inches taller than Godwin.

"No," said Jill. "I was standing close enough to touch him."

"Stooped down, you mean."

"No, standing up straight."

"And close enough to touch me *right on the tush*," Godwin confided in a low voice, rounding his eyes and feigning shock.

"I was reaching for his belt," corrected Jill.

"Could you see me?" Betsy asked Jill.

"Not once I got behind Godwin. I saw you coming out of a suite and told Godwin to get your attention and stepped behind him. I couldn't see you, and figured you couldn't see me, either. And I was right. If you had been on six, or even five, we probably would have seen each other."

"But that means . . ." Betsy gestured.

"Yes," said Jill. "That means that you and Samantha Mills wouldn't have seen someone standing behind Belle, even if he or she were close enough to touch her. To grab and lift her over."

"But surely I would have seen something, an arm or a hand!" Betsy turned and leaned against the railing. "It's too high to just push someone over, see? You'd have to grab and lift."

"Yes, that's true," said Jill.

Godwin said, "This is like high school math. If we knew how tall Belle was, maybe we could figure out the height limits of the person who pushed her over."

"She was short, about five four," Jill said.

Betsy said, "But my question remains: How could she get lifted over the railing without my seeing an arm or a hand on her?"

"I have an idea for a way to figure that out," said Jill. "She wasn't as tall as you," she continued, looking at Godwin. "But I'm taller than most, so we'll use me and you. Betsy, go back down three flights and look up here."

"What are you going to do?" asked Godwin, who, knowing Jill, was not as alarmed as he should have been, in Betsy's opinion.

"Well, I would toss you over in various ways, but after the first couple of times you wouldn't be worth much as a model. Besides, people are upset enough as it is."

"Well, thank you very much!" said Godwin, "But what *are* you going to do?"

"Now don't you worry your pretty little head," said Jill as she put her hands on Godwin's shoulders, either reassuringly or to prevent his escape. "Go on, go on," she said to Betsy.

Betsy hurried to the stairwell, keeping her smile to herself until out of sight. Jill was a staid, even proper sort of person, except on rare occasions when a weird sense of fun broke a seal and erupted. This seemed to be one of those times. Godwin was, of course, safe as houses, and would surely realize that on some level. Betsy hoped it was a conscious one.

She came out on the sixth floor and hurried up along the gallery walk to near the elevator, where she turned and looked up. Godwin grinned and waved and Jill, visible beside him, suddenly vanished from sight. An instant later Godwin rose as if on a jet of water. Jill's arm was visible around his waist and as his legs came into sight, her other arm was visible around one of them just above knee level. Godwin's mouth opened, but Jill appeared to say something to him, and no sound came out. He sank back down again, and Jill appeared beside him.

Betsy shook her head no. That wasn't at all what she had seen.

"What are they doing up there?" came a woman's voice, startling her. Betsy turned to see a stout Asian woman with beautiful silver streaks in her black hair looking from Betsy to Jill and Godwin then back again.

"It's kind of an experiment."

"It looks like skylarking, and if they're not careful, someone else is going to fall off that railing, and then where will we be? I think I'll go to the front desk and warn them about this."

"It's not skylarking, it's serious. That woman up there is a police officer, and she's trying to figure out how the dead woman fell."

The Asian woman watched Jill arranging Godwin at the top of the railing in a new way, then said, "Well, if it's police business, I suppose they must know what they are doing."

She went on her way, and Betsy waved at Jill to continue the experiment. Other people stopped as it went on, but all accepted the explanation that it was a police experiment to see how Belle came to fall. What people stopping to look from other places must have thought, Betsy wondered.

Several failing combinations later, Godwin stood panting, with his hands braced on the railing well away from his body. He turned his head as if to protest where Jill's grip had landed this time and one hand came off the railing. Then the rest of his upper body slipped forward and suddenly he seemed about to go over entirely. Betsy gasped and would have let the breath out in a scream but Godwin was grabbed by the shoulder of his sweater and pulled back.

This time when Jill appeared at the railing; Betsy, still openmouthed, nodded. That was what Betsy had seen when it was Belle at the railing just before her fall.

Godwin, looking shaken but grinning bravely, waved at her to come up.

When Betsy arrived on six, she found a small crowd around Jill and Godwin. Two were hotel employees, marked by their white shirts, black trousers, and the blue laminated ID cards on lanyards around their necks. Some of the others were committee members, the rest were shop-owners. All were looking alarmed and speaking sharply.

"I guess people do pay attention to what goes on above the shopping floors," Godwin said, sidling out of the crowd and up to Betsy. "They're pretty definite that the experiment is over."

"Well, it doesn't matter. That last try was the one. How did Jill do it?"

"Stooped and grabbed me by the lower legs. Lifted and pushed forward, all in one motion. It was almost too easy; think I might have gone over if she hadn't grabbed me back."

Betsy looked over at Jill, who was looking a little winded and thought perhaps it only felt easy. Godwin was not by any means a heavyweight, but Jill had lifted him six or seven times in fewer than that many minutes. Of course, the murderer had only to do it once . . .

Betsy moved closer to the crowd and heard Jill saying, "Yes, of course. It was a necessary experiment, but we're done now, and it won't be repeated."

"Well, all right," said a committee member, somewhat grudgingly.

"I'm going to hold you to that," said another.

"*Thank* you," said a tall black woman Betsy recognized as the desk clerk. She seemed to be holding in her anger with much effort, biting off the words.

The crowd slowly broke up and Jill came to Betsy. "What do you think now?" she asked.

"What you did to Godwin last is what I saw happen to Belle. What can I say? It sure seems to be murder."

Fifteen

Jill, Godwin, and Betsy went back to their suite. "Where do we start?" Jill asked Betsy.

"You're asking me?"

"You're the one who solves murders," said Jill. "If we were trying to arrest a drunk driver now, or deciding how to arrange the watch list so Mike could take his vacation, then you'd be asking me for advice."

Betsy looked around for something to write on. Jill picked up a couple of sheets of hotel stationery, but Betsy waved them off. "I need a notebook or tablet. I always lose the most important sheet of a stack of loose paper," she said.

Then she saw the Management and Hiring booklet. She picked it up and opened it. As she remembered, the sets of rules were one-sided; the back of each page was blank. "This will do fine," she said. She found a pen in her purse, but hesitated before clicking the point out. "I don't like this."

"Why not?" asked Jill.

"Well, suppose this *is* a suicide?"

Jill frowned lightly at her. "But you didn't see her throw a leg over the railing, or hoist herself up on her arms," she said.

"No . . . no, you're right. But how about those railings? Maybe stepping up on the rail along the bottom gave her enough height to, I don't know, sort of lean over and keep going."

Godwin said, "How far off the floor is the bottom railing?"

Jill started for the door to the suite. "Come on, let's see."

They went out into the gallery and up to the railing, where Betsy—with Jill holding onto her sweater in back and Godwin standing with both fists pressed nervously against his jaw—stood on the bottom rail and tried to lean over. She tried it flat footed, on her toes and by leaning a little sideways. But the bottom rail didn't lift her high enough.

"Satisfied?" asked Jill after three tries.

"Yeah, I guess so."

They had only taken two steps back toward the suite when Betsy said, "Uh-oh."

"What?" asked Jill.

"Look who's coming."

Coming swiftly toward them was Marveen Harrison, de facto manager. Betsy was put in mind of a film she had once seen, of a tornado rolling with terrifying power and big cracks of electricity through power lines toward a helpless farm.

"I'm sorry—" Betsy began as soon as Marveen came within earshot, but Marveen was having none of it.

"Listen to me, the three of you," she said in a low voice that had a distinct growl of thunder in it. "I *believe* in cooperating with the authorities, and I have given you *all the latitude* I could in doing whatever you think needs to be done. But *this*—!" She gestured at the railing. "I *thought* I had a promise from you that you would stop alarming the other guests in this hotel with your shenanigans."

"Yes, ma'am, you did," said Jill. "But there was one more—"

"*No*," said Marveen with great firmness. "There is *nothing more*. You may talk to anyone you like, you may poke and pry all you want, but you are *not* to climb, crawl, clamber, *or* jump over, throw over, or *pretend* to throw something or *some one* over any more railings, is that clear?"

"Yes, of course," said Betsy humbly.

"Yes'm," mumbled Godwin.

"Yes, ma'am," said Jill firmly.

"Humph," said Marveen, giving them one more good scratch with her eyes. She turned and stalked away.

"Whew," said Godwin, when she was out of earshot. "I guess she told us."

"Well, we certainly asked for it." said Betsy. "Come on." She led the way back to their room.

Once inside, Jill asked, "Where were we?"

"I don't know," said Betsy tiredly. "I wish I did know." She sat down at the round table to stare disconsolate at the booklet.

"I think I know what's wrong here," Jill said.

"What?" asked Betsy.

"This isn't like back home, where you know the town

and the people. Nor is this like your usual setup, where someone comes to you for help because an innocent person has been accused of wrongdoing."

Betsy nodded. "Yes, you're right. I feel as if I'm working blind, as if I'll never come close to solving this. I think we should quit. I have another important mission here. This is a once-a-year opportunity to see, handle and buy the latest in needlework supplies, charts, and gadgets. I have an obligation to my shop and my customers to do that."

"Now wait," said Godwin. "I can do the rest of the buying, if you'll trust me. I know counted isn't my strong suit, but I've worked in Crewel World longer than you have, and I've got a feel for what our customers like."

"I do trust you, Goddy, but it's important for me to see what's out there, too."

"Yeah, I know, but——" He gestured at the book she was resting her hand on.

Jill said, "He's right. This is important, too. Maybe more important. Please try, Betsy. Pretend for a couple of minutes that you've got the time to investigate. Where would you start?"

"Well . . ." Betsy sat down and opened the booklet to stroke the blank left page with her palm, preparing to write on it. Her eye was caught by the first rule printed on the right in thick black type: "Always document problems as they occur, as well as what you have done to alter the problem."

"Huh," she said, "this applies to us in this situation, too," and read it aloud.

"See?" said Jill, a bit dryly, "Even Susan Stinner thinks thinks you should do this."

"Define terms, define terms!" said Godwin, and when they looked at him he said, "Well, isn't that what we have to do? That's what John says is the correct way to begin solving a problem."

"I think we should begin by defining the problem," said Betsy.

"The problem is," said Jill, "someone murdered Belle Hammermill, and since the local police aren't here to solve it, we should."

"Why?" demanded Betsy.

"Because, unlike anyone else here, you have an established track record for amateur sleuthing."

Betsy sighed. "All right," she grumbled and wrote at the top of the blank page, "Who killed Belle Hammermill?"

"We have three suspects," said Jill. "Cherry Pye, Eve Suttle, and Lenore King."

Betsy wrote their names down, numbering them one, two, and three. Then she put a big capital A under Cherry's name. "Goddy, tell me again about your conversation with Ms. Pye."

Godwin, seeing the importance of this question, took half a minute to organize his thoughts. "She was really upset when I saw her. I mean, she wasn't fake-crying—she was really crying. There were real tears, and she kept blowing her nose . . . you know . . ." He thought for a bit, groping for the right adverb, and finally produced, "juicily."

"Good, that's good," nodded Jill.

"Ish," noted Betsy, not writing that down.

"It may be gross, but it's a rare actor who can produce snot at will." So Betsy dutifully wrote, *Real tears and snot.*

"What did she say, Goddy?" asked Jill.

"Remember I already told you that she said Belle was more absentminded than usual? That she would forget to order things or order the wrong things? Well, I've got something to add to that. I was in Doug Kreinik's suite first thing this morning, looking at their iron-on ribbon, and I heard him talking to a Hoffman rep. He told the Hoffman guy Belle Hammermill ordered some Kreinik product COD, then told the UPS man to wait when it arrived, while she went in back to empty the box, close it up again and mark it refused."

Betsy stared at him. "He said *Belle Hammermill* did this?"

Godwin nodded. "By name. Doug told the Hoffman guy to spread the word to other suppliers not to take any order from her without cash in advance. Later, I heard someone in the Weichelt suite talking about it, so I asked if Mr. Kreinik had told her this himself, and she said yes. Then someone else jumped in to say that now Belle is dead, he had stopped spreading the word about her since it didn't matter anymore."

"I wonder where he was when Belle died?" Jill remarked in a dry voice.

"Talking to Dave Stott," said Godwin seriously.

"She's kidding, for heaven's sake, Goddy," said Betsy.

"How do you know I'm kidding?" Jill said, not sounding as if she was kidding.

Betsy said, "Because I was in Norden Crafts awhile ago and Dave was looking kind of sad so I asked him if he knew Belle Hammermill and he said, 'Just in passing,' and his wife threw a pillow at him. She explained that he was talking to Doug when they both saw Belle go by into the atrium." Goddy turned to frown at Jill, then he caught the merest tweak of one corner of her mouth, and giggled.

"Honestly, Goddy!" scolded Betsy. "How you can even

think—" Doug Kreinik had come to Crewel World a year ago to give an evening talk on his company's products to Betsy and a group of her customers, including Jill, and proven himself a bright, entertaining, personable representative of his company. He also positively reeked of integrity.

Jill said, "Still, we have a motive and an alibi for Doug Kreinik. Write it down." She had the tweak under control, but not the twinkle in her light blue eyes.

Betsy said, "Jill, you have the weirdest sense of humor." And deliberately turning a shoulder to it, she asked Godwin, "Did Cherry hint that she knew Belle was doing something dishonest?"

"No, not that I could tell."

"Well, was she angry or resentful about Belle's airheadedness?"

Godwin thought some more. "I don't think so," he said. "You have to realize, she was such a mess, it was hard to tell anything else about her. All I could see was that she was crying over the horrible death of her business partner. Wait a minute, wait a minute, maybe she did say something . . ." He fell into a studied silence. "It was about not liking Belle," he said after nearly a minute. "No, that wasn't the word, it was . . . *fond*. Yes, she said, 'I wasn't very fond of Belle lately.' " He sat up straight and beamed at them. "Now that's a *memory* for you!"

"Very good, Goddy," said Jill. She added, to Betsy, "Think about it. If I'd just tossed someone over a railing and hoped to get away with it, I'd be telling people what good friends we were. So *because* she admitted she wasn't 'fond' of Belle that would indicate she's probably not the murderer."

"Yes," Betsy said, "but it's still odd. In a moment like that, crying over the horrible death of someone I worked with, was partners with, I'd think all I could talk about was the good stuff."

"Are we going to talk to her, then?" asked Godwin.

"Oh, yes." Betsy nodded. "If for no other reason than to ask her if she knows someone who was seriously angry with Belle." She tapped her pen on the page she'd been writing on. "There's a lot we don't know."

"We know Cherry Pye was really upset," said Godwin.

"So was Eve Suttle," said Betsy, remembering the stammer, the copious tears, the helplessly-quaking shoulders. She made a note.

"Where was it you saw her sitting down and crying?" asked Jill.

"Eighth floor, on the long side, about halfway from the end and the elevators."

"Which end?"

Betsy thought. "Well, we're on the short side above the lobby, and I was going from there to the elevators, so along there." She nodded to herself and wrote that down, then tapped the writing with the pen. "She said something about going down twice."

"In the elevator?"

"No, the stairs. Not down, around. She said she went around twice."

Godwin snorted. "What does that mean?"

"Each floor has a landing between," said Jill. "You go down, cross a landing, and go down again, to go down one floor." She and Betsy exchanged looks.

"Oh, right," said Godwin, baffled. "Well, look, if we're going to talk to Cherry, we should get going, shouldn't we?"

"Not yet," said Betsy. "And anyway, Goddy, I don't think you should come with us."

"Why not?" He looked almost comically disappointed.

"Well, there's this little matter of the Market. I guess you're going to have to be the Crewel World buyer for the rest of today, while Jill and I do this."

Godwin blinked at her, a smile starting to form. "For real? Go to all the floors, make my own decisions?"

"For real. Whoops, wait a second." She hurried back into the bedroom to find her purse and extract the Market Guide. She came back and handed it to him. "I've marked the suppliers I particularly wanted to visit. Other than that, you're on your own. Go, boy."

"Oh, joy!" He took the little booklet and stuffed it behind his belt. Then he whipped out his Visa card, held it up like a sword, and crowed, "Chaaaaaaaarge!" And he was out the door.

Once he was gone, Jill said, "When did you get the Market Guide?"

"It was in the packet we got when we checked in on arrival," said Betsy. "Why?"

"It didn't come in advance?"

"No, I think they didn't know until the last minute who all was coming. Why?"

"Seeing that guide marked up made me remember seeing another one falling out of Belle's purse beside her body. She must've gotten hers on checking in, too. And marked it up last night or this morning."

"Yes. So?"

"I remember thinking at the time that people who are going to commit suicide don't plan a shopping trip."

Betsy tossed the pen down. "We didn't need to go

climbing all over that railing, getting Marveen Harrison mad at us, did we?"

"No, I guess not. Sorry."

Betsy sighed and picked the pen back up. "Eve said 'coming down the stairs'."

"Yes."

"She went right away into talking about taking the elevator to the wrong floor, but first she said 'coming down the stairs,' which makes me think she walked down from nine. Jill, have you ever talked to someone who committed a murder and was sorry?"

A faint emotion crossed Jill's face, too swift to be read. "No, but I've talked to people who have talked to them. Which makes it hearsay. Still, for what it's worth, some have reported tears and regret. Now I remember someone who accidentally ran over a neighbor with his car. In my case, the man cried real tears, too. But what happened here today wasn't an accident."

"No. But suppose it was an impulse. You're angry at Belle, you wish something bad would happen to her—and there she is, leaning over a railing. You walk over, lift, and she's gone. You could do it in three seconds, without thinking, and then be shocked and horrified. And dreadfully sorry."

Jill considered this, and nodded. "All right, yes."

"That would fit both Eve and Cherry, wouldn't it?" Betsy touched the third name on her list. "You talked to Lenore King at lunch today."

"With you watching."

"Yes, but I didn't know this was murder, so I wasn't paying the same kind of attention you were. Anyway, you've talked with people in trouble often enough. What did you think of Lenore?"

"She was upset, but in a different way, not crying," said Jill slowly. "And denying she murdered Belle before anyone even asked is strange, don't you think?"

Betsy made a note of that. "Yes. Does she have an alibi?"

"That's something we'll have to find out. I hope so; it would be nice to eliminate just one of these people."

Betsy made a note and closed the booklet. "So let's go talk to someone. Who first?"

"The first one on the list. Cherry Pye."

Sixteen

Saturday, 4:17 P.M.

Jill and Betsy took the clanging, echoing stairs up to nine and went down the hall to Cherry's suite, which was a few doors short of the spot where Belle went over the railing. Jill knocked.

Fairly quickly, the door opened, and there sat a woman in a wheelchair. She had short, light-brown hair, tumbled attractively around a pretty face set with smokey-green eyes under level brows. She wore a loose-fitting knit shirt of royal purple, lavender slacks, and new-looking white walking shoes with velcro fasteners.

"Yes?" she inquired.

Jill spoke first. "I'm Jill Cross Larson, a police sergeant from Minnesota."

For the merest instant, Cherry's face paled, but the color came back. "Minnesota?" she said.

"Yes. I've volunteered to assist the local police by collecting information about Belle Hammermill."

"But Belle was from Wisconsin."

"I know. I'm collecting this information for the Nashville police."

Almost laughing, she pursued, "But . . . Minnesota?" She gestured widely, meaning they were surrounded by Tennessee, whose border did not come anywhere near Minnesota.

Jill smiled faintly. "Yes, Minnesota. I came to Nashville for a police seminar and got caught up in this by accident. I took a couple of friends out to dinner last night, and had such a terrible time getting them back to this hotel that they insisted I stay."

"I bet you're sorry about that," said Cherry, her face gone grim.

"Well, I've had happier times. May we come in?" Jill took half a step forward.

But Cherry didn't move back for her. Instead she frowned and looked at Betsy. "Who's she, another cop?" Her tone was sarcastic.

"No," said Betsy, "I'm one of the dinner friends. I'm Betsy Devonshire, and I own a store back in Excelsior, Minnesota."

"She takes good notes," said Jill mildly, and Betsy held out the Hiring and Management booklet, already turned to a new blank page.

Cherry started to smile, but decided she was still puzzled. So Jill continued to explain. "Nashville PD has pretty

much decided Belle's death was due to an unfortunate accident. The problem is, they are really swamped by this blizzard, lots of far more urgent calls: serious accidents, power
lines down, and so forth. They'd conduct these interviews
themselves if that wasn't the case. You knew Ms. Hammermill well, didn't you?"

"Yes, of course." Her face went sad. "She was my . . .
partner in business. All right, come in." As she turned and
wheeled away Betsy was struck by the smooth and powerful
movement of her arms and shoulders.

Cherry wheeled around in the center of the room and
gestured at the couch. Her voice and expression were suddenly pleasant, a hostess greeting welcome guests, as she
asked, "Care to sit down?"

Betsy was beginning to get whiplash of the mind, following Cherry's sudden shifts in mood. But Jill merely said,
"Yes, thank you. Oh, but is it all right if we sit over here?"
Jill went to draw back a chair at a round table under a swag
lamp, a twin to the one in their own suite. "The light's better, and Betsy can use the table to write on."

"Sure, all right."

But Betsy thought she knew of another reason: With
everyone in chairs, their heads would all be on one level. It's
hard to control a conversation with someone who is looking
down on you, as Cherry would on them sitting on the couch.
She'd read that in a Travis McGee novel a long time ago—
it's possible to learn real things from fiction. Though Betsy
was willing to bet Jill hadn't learned it from a novel.

"Would you like coffee?" Cherry asked them, still the
hostess. The sitting room was full of the smell of freshly
brewed coffee and a pot of it was sitting in its maker on the
narrow counter beside the sink.

"Why, yes, thank you," said Jill, who drank coffee all day long, even at bedtime. "Black, please," she added.

"No, thank you," said Betsy, who couldn't sleep if she indulged in caffeine after two o'clock. It was nearly five. She wrote Cherry's name at the top of the page and below it wrote, *Volatile.*

Cherry brought a mug for Jill and filled a second for herself. "Now," she said, wrapping her hand around her mug rather than holding it by the handle, "what did you want to ask me about Belle?"

Jill said, "Something else first: You've probably been asked a thousand times—"

"Yes, it's my real name," the woman interrupted, her smile gone sour. She spread her lower arms in a gesture half shrug, half invitation—but gently, so as not to slosh. "And it's okay to laugh, really it is. Though I wish my parents had at least thought to give me a middle name, in case I didn't think their joke was funny. Which I don't. Because then I wouldn't have a problem every time someone asks me my name." She shook her head, her mouth still pulled back in that painful smile. "But at least it's not the kind of name people forget as soon as they hear it."

"You're right there," said Betsy, looking down at her open notebook, away from the pain. She wrote: *Hates her name.* On the side opposite the blank page was Rule 6: "Reward, reward, reward—and praise!" So she added, "And it's not a bad name, really. Sweet, cheerful, down-home and delicious. Cherry pie is on just about everyone's list of favorites."

Cherry cocked her head at Betsy, judging her, then smiled. "Thank you," she said, drawing the words out a little to emphasize she was really pleased, and took a sip of coffee.

Jill asked, "Did you and Belle arrive together at the Market?"

Cherry nodded. "We flew in Friday evening. We'd decided not to take any classes this year."

Betsy asked, "Does Belle have any relatives who need to be told?"

Cherry paused to take a breath that was nearly a sob. "Well, she has a sister named Cassy and a brother, I think his name is Eliot. I don't know where they live—not in Wisconsin, I know that. Her parents are dead. There isn't a husband—at least, she's divorced. It was a long time ago, no kids. There's an aunt and an uncle . . ." Cherry, eyes half closed, had been nodding at each person named in her recitation while Betsy made swift notes. She opened them again, and Betsy saw their green had gone from a soft Anchor 261 to something nearly gray—maybe 1040?

"I didn't know what to do. You see, I can't get home. So what I did was, I e-mailed our attorney, and asked him to notify her relatives, since I don't know how to from here. I have the information—at home. In a drawer. I kept meaning to put it into my computer, but never did. It should have occurred to me, I suppose, that I might need that information away from home. You know, emergency contact numbers." She glanced toward the door to the bedroom. "I use the same laptop at home and on the road, so my computer's right in there." She looked at Jill. "Was that the right thing to do? I hate to think of a lawyer calling these people to tell them. That sounds kind of cold."

"You did fine," said Jill. "And you're being very helpful to us. How long did you know Belle?"

"I met her nine or ten years ago, when she was working

in the shop we ended up buying. That was before my accident. We were partners almost five years. I saw her almost every day during those five years."

"So you were friends?" asked Betsy.

Cherry blinked several times, as if surprised at the question, took another sip of her coffee, then nodded. "Of course."

Betsy wrote, *Liar?* and asked, "What was she like?"

Cherry thought a moment, then smiled. "There's a word someone used once, and it was just right. 'Vivacious.' That was Belle. Smart and full of energy. And she was sweet—and funny, mostly making fun of herself. Good with customers. People really liked her."

"Did she have *any* faults?" Betsy got just the right tone, making it sound as if Belle must be exaggerating this paragon.

Cherry's smile faded. "Nobody's perfect, of course." She looked at her hands. Jill inhaled softly, as if to ask something, but Betsy, turning over a page in the booklet, jogged her elbow and she exhaled again without speaking.

After a few moments, Cherry said, "Okay, she was kind of airheaded, forgetting to order things for customers, or messing up an order—but she made jokes about it, like she'd say her brain must be made out of a sieve; and customers couldn't stay mad at her for more than a minute."

Betsy smiled and nodded, writing. "I'll remember that for next time I mess up in my shop."

Jill said, "Now, about today. Do you think what happened to her was an accident?"

"Why sure, what else could it be?"

"Well, those railings are kind of high for a person to go over by accident."

"They are? I thought they were kind of low."

Betsy asked, "How tall was Belle?"

"Five foot, three and three-quarters. She thought it was cute to say that, rather than rounding up to five four."

"I'm five four," said Betsy. She half stood. "The railing comes up to here on me." She held her forearm horizontally across her lower ribs, then sat down again. "I couldn't go over by accident unless I was standing on something and leaned over too far." She looked inquiringly at Cherry, who widened her eyes at her in surprise.

"You mean like standing on a chair?" Cherry considered that with a doubtful expression, and then shook her head.

"Can you stand?" Jill asked abruptly.

Cherry's attention swiveled back to her. "If I have something to hang onto, like a bar, or crutches. I can stand alone in water, if it's deep enough. But I can't walk. I have feeling in my legs, but I can't move them. Oh, I see what you're getting at. If I try to stand, I fall over easily, so maybe I'm— what do you call it—projecting."

"Yes, possibly," said Jill. "But you see how there may be a problem, trying to figure out how Belle went over the railing by accident."

"Yes. Yes, I can see that now."

"But what about suicide?" asked Betsy.

Cherry turned to Betsy, her eyes green again. "Yes, what about that? Do you think—?" She wheeled forward, all the way to the table, to put her coffee cup on it, let her hand rest on the cup a moment or two, then pulled it back into her lap. "Because she *was* different lately. Preoccupied, I guess that's the word. Not really unhappy, not what I'd call *depressed*, but something was wrong. She didn't say what, but something was wrong. So maybe—maybe yes, it could be suicide."

Betsy wrote, *Agrees it might be suicide.*

Jill asked, "Where were you when you learned she was dead?"

Cherry drew her shoulders up and her eyes wandered around the room. "In an elevator." She touched her chin with her fingertips, and her eyes came back to Jill. "I mean, I was just passing by the Kreinik suite—it was too crowded for me to get in there—when I heard the yell and the . . . the smash, but I thought it was a prank, someone dropping something to get a rise out of us. Or a banner falling. I never thought it could be a person. People were excited and rushing around, but I didn't want to go gaping like a tourist, so I refused to pay any attention. Then in the elevator I heard someone . . . say it was a person who fell and she was . . . dead, and I looked then, and recognized—" Cherry cut herself off with a gesture, and a big sob escaped her. "Excuse me." She turned and rolled swiftly toward the bathroom, nicking the extra-wide doorway on her way through with the axle of her chair.

They heard the sound of sobbing, then of a nose being blown, then water running. In another minute Cherry came back, a couple of clean tissues in her lap, looking almost angry.

"This isn't like me!" she said harshly. "Normally I can handle anything! But every time I think about seeing her like that, I just . . . go to pieces."

Betsy, the image rising unbidden behind her eyes, said, "It's horrible to see anyone dead from a big fall. And to see someone you know all broken, that must be terribly difficult."

Cherry's mouth thinned with distress. "Yes, it was." She looked down at her lap, and said softly, "And yet, on the other hand, I keep forgetting it happened. Like, this is my third time here in Nashville, and everything else is so familiar that I keep thinking Belle will come in here and tell me to quit goofing off talking to people and get back to buying." Cherry's face suddenly twisted and she put the heels of her hands up to her eyes. "Sorry . . . sorry."

She shifted her hands so they covered her face, and continued in a muffled, angry voice, "Could you find out when they're going to take her away? I can't *stand* their leaving her down on the floor like that!"

Jill said, "That's been taken care of. An ambulance crew managed to climb the hill on foot a couple of hours ago."

"Oh?" Cherry brought her hands down to show a surprised blank. "I didn't know that," she said. "I went down for lunch and saw she was still there, and I came right back up here and didn't go out again. So I didn't know." She looked around the room, as if for the complaint she had unexpectedly been relieved of. "Where . . . where did they take her?"

"I'm sure they're holding the body at the morgue in case they decide to do an autopsy."

"Why? I mean, if they thought it was an accident . . ."

"Well, they're probably going to wait until I report in," said Jill. "And I'm quite sure it wasn't an accident. So let's continue. How did you come to be partners?"

Cherry looked at her for a few moments, a little surprised. But Jill had asked another question and now she hastened to answer it.

"I was looking to invest some of the money I got in a settlement after my accident. A lot of it went into safe places, but I'm young and I plan to live to a ripe old age, so I want to grow my money. Belle had worked in this shop for a long time, and I came in a lot so we knew each other. She told me it was for sale, but she didn't have the money to buy it. Every time I came in, there were other customers, especially on weekends. She thought it was a good investment, and so did I."

"But it wasn't?"

"Well, not as good as I hoped. I guess I didn't understand that owning a small business isn't exactly like planting a money tree."

"You got that right," Betsy said in a dry voice.

Cherry made a sound like a chuckle being strangled at birth, then cleared her throat and became serious. "This is so strange," she said.

"What is?" asked Betsy.

"We're sitting here making jokes about owning a business, and at the same time we're talking about Belle's death. And you—" she looked at Jill "—you're saying it wasn't an accident. Do you really think it was suicide?"

"Seriously? No."

Cherry's mouth opened, but then she froze. "*No?* What do you mean, no?"

"I mean I'm not sure it was a suicide, either."

The color drained from Cherry's face, and she looked at Betsy. "What does she mean?" she asked, though it was obvious she knew the answer.

"She means she thinks Belle might have been murdered."

"*No!*" shouted Cherry. "That's impossible!" She turned on Jill, angry and frightened. "You're crazy! All of a sudden you're talking like you're crazy! This is stupid, I can't listen to this! You're going to have to leave, right now!"

"All right." Jill stood.

Betsy didn't stand, but said, "You know, if someone

murdered Belle, I'd think you'd want to know who. And, since you were her partner, why."

"Why?" Cherry echoed. Her puzzled frown suddenly smoothed away. "Oh, *why*. I hadn't thought of that. Maybe you shouldn't go, then. Maybe I could keep answering your questions."

And Betsy made another brief note: *Scared.*

Seventeen

Saturday, 4:28 P.M.

Jill turned back, sat down, and asked, "Was anyone you know mad at Belle?"

There was a pause, then Cherry murmured, "God, I hate this." She sighed and wrung her hands, and Betsy was struck by the play of powerful muscles in her forearms. "All right. Like I said, Belle was a bit of an airhead. She made it cute, part of her charm, but it sometimes meant things didn't get done and customers would be disappointed."

"Any customer in particular?"

"Well, Judy Neville, who was supposed to bring a marriage sampler to a friend's wedding, but Belle put the due date down wrong and it wasn't ready on time. Judy was angry and said she wasn't going to bring anything else to us to be finished ever again. She was pretty steamed about it."

"I don't suppose Judy Neville is here at the Market today," mused Betsy, and Cherry laughed uncomfortably and agreed that she wasn't.

"We mean someone here at Market who was angry at Belle," persisted Jill.

"Yes, I know, I understand," said Cherry. She wheeled back a foot and forward again. "Lenore King," she said at last. "She's here and she's pretty upset."

Betsy wrote the name down while Jill said, "She's the one with the Christmas tree sampler, isn't she?"

"Yes. Have you seen her model? It's kind of a mess."

"And she blames Belle for that," suggested Jill, glancing at Betsy, who flashed her a replying look meaning *yes, yes, I understand.* She had no intention of letting Cherry know they'd already talked with Lenore.

"Yes. And she's right, it was Belle's fault. Lenore brought her model to us in early August, before INRG announced the change of date. God, it was a beautiful thing, you could see that even when it was in eight pieces. So Belle sent it to Marj with a February 4 due date. Then the Market got changed to December." Cherry drew a breath and let it out, and said, reluctantly, "And Belle didn't call Marj to tell her Lenore needed that piece before Lenore left for Nashville. She knew, she had to know; Lenore had done nothing but talk about how she was going to introduce it at Market. She bragged about how Bewitching Stitches was going to publish the pattern, and worried over how it had to sell well if she wanted to become a professional pattern designer. So every employee and regular at Samplers and More knew this was happening at Market, we even had customers talking about it when Lenore wasn't there."

"Did Lenore come in and specifically tell Belle that she needed the pattern in December instead of February?" asked Betsy.

Cherry started to smile, but it got twisted up in her look of exasperation and distress. "No, she came in and told *me*. I wrote a note to Belle and put it on the checkout counter right beside the phone. She told Lenore she never saw the note."

Betsy nodded as she wrote, *Same story*. Meaning it agreed with what Lenore had said.

"Well, then it seems to me the person Lenore would be mad at is you," Jill pointed out.

"And it would have been if Lenore hadn't watched me write the note and put it where Belle couldn't have missed it. I think it annoyed Belle just a little that she couldn't make me share the blame." This time the smile won, if barely.

"Did she do that once in awhile?" Betsy asked. "Dump the blame on you?" Her tone was sympathetic.

"No!" said Cherry, too sharply. She realized that and winced, then amended, "Oh, all right, once in awhile," her tone reluctant. "Sometimes I would think she was like the half the population that believes people with spinal cord injuries have major brain-cell loss, too." She shrugged. "But then she'd do something so nice, so sweet, I'd remember that we really were partners, and we'd be friends again."

Jill asked, "Is it possible Belle deliberately failed to contact your finisher about Lenore's model?"

Cherry hesitated. "Why would she do that?"

"Maybe because there was a quarrel of some sort," suggested Betsy, "between Lenore and Belle."

Jill turned to Betsy. "That can't be right, Betsy, because

if there was, she could've taken it to some other finisher."

"No, for two reasons," said Cherry. "First, we're the only cross-stitch shop in Milwaukee. Second, we have a wonderful finisher. People who move away will sometimes mail us projects for Marj to finish. I'm sure it wasn't on purpose, it's just that once in a while Belle would mess up. This time it turned out really, really bad for Lenore."

"Up to that point, had Belle been encouraging Lenore's efforts?" Betsy asked.

"Oh, yes. She put some of her early patterns in our newsletter, and helped her find a good computer program to print out new ones, and encouraged her to enter her work in competitions. Then as Lenore improved, she made copies of her patterns, to give to customers as freebies. And later she was all cheers for Lenore when she sold a pattern to a magazine. But then Lenore got this idea for a Christmas tree sampler, and when Belle saw how great it really was, all she could do was criticize it. If Lenore hadn't brought it to a guild meeting and heard all the raves, she might not have sent it to Bewitching Stitches."

Betsy asked, "You think it was sabotage?"

Cherry nodded wordlessly.

"But why would Belle do that? Had Lenore done something to make her angry?"

Cherry sighed and didn't reply right away. But Jill and Betsy held their tongues as well, so Cherry said, "This is hard to explain. Belle liked helping people, she really did. But if they shaped up better than she thought they would, you know, became actually successful, she was . . . like jealous, or something. Does that sound too weird?"

"It sounds like something that might happen, I suppose," Jill said doubtfully.

But Betsy nodded and said, "Oh, yes." She'd seen it in action once, long ago, in a college professor.

Cherry continued, "It's like she would bust her buns to help people, but it's also like she wanted them to always be needing her help. And she'd find a reason to run them off if they didn't need her help anymore."

"Not a nice person," Betsy murmured.

Cherry's face twisted in pain and she said, "No, she *was* a nice person! I want you to understand, this hardly ever happened! People would take her help, and move on, grateful. Others . . . Well, most people who are a mess stay a mess, you know!"

Betsy, amused at this hard truth baldly stated, said, "Yes, I know."

"So Belle could be patient and nice and helpful all she wanted, and they'd stay grateful and hopeful. It was nice of Belle, even though it was also kind of like a game she almost never lost."

"Nice of Belle, but not a very nice game," said Jill.

Cherry sighed. "Well, maybe not. But like I said, she didn't end up running people off very often."

"Was Lenore a mess?" Betsy asked.

"Yes, but not a bad one. She wanted to stay home with her kids, and the only talent she had that might let her do that was stitching. No one, not even Lenore, ever thought she could design patterns well enough to earn any money at it, not until Belle started encouraging her to think so. And then all of a sudden, Lenore comes up with this gangbuster idea. Belle told me it was a great idea but that Lenore would never be able to work it out, because it was too complicated. But she kept encouraging Lenore to keep trying. And then, what do you know, Lenore solves all the problems and finishes her charts of it. And it's fabulous! Belle told her it needed more work, but Lenore sends it off to Bewitching Stitches and they like it. So then Belle says Bewitching might try to cheat her, that maybe she should take it back and try selling it to a magazine, but by then, everyone else was cheering her on. And Lenore was getting excited about another sampler idea."

"Did you think to warn Lenore about Belle's little game?" asked Betsy.

"No. Because I didn't really realize she was playing it on Lenore until the model didn't come back on time. The look on Lenore's face . . . She, she was just . . . *demolished*. But the look on Belle's . . ." Cherry rubbed her cheeks with both hands. "It was weird. It was sick." She looked shamefaced at Betsy. "But I didn't say anything, not to either of them. I couldn't think what to say."

"If you knew how important this was, and you knew about this problem with Belle, why didn't you call Marj yourself?" asked Jill.

Cherry snapped, "I *told* you, I didn't know Belle was going to do that to Lenore!" She took a calming breath. "And anyway, finishing was separate from Samplers and More. Belle kept the records, drew up the bills, and split the money it made with Marj. It was its own business, and not a part of Samplers and More."

"That's funny, that isn't the way it works in my shop," said Betsy.

"No? Well, I thought it was odd; but Belle said it was better for tax purposes, and anyway the old owner did it that way, too," said Cherry.

Betsy, making a note, said, "The name of your shop is

Belle's Samplers and More, and she kept a part of it separate from you. How much of a partner were you in the business?"

"Fifty-fifty!" Cherry said sharply, almost angrily. "I told you, I put up the money, Belle brought the expertise!" She heard the tone of her voice and, with a visible effort, unclenched her jaw.

"We went back and forth about the name. The original owner's name for the store was Samplers and More. I thought keeping the old name would be a good thing, since she had a good customer base, but Belle wanted to call it The Silver Thimble. So we cut cards to see who got to name the store, and she won. And instead of a new name, she called it *Belle's* Samplers and More. She called it a compromise, but my name didn't go on the sign, only hers."

"Were you angry about that?"

Cherry laughed harshly. "Oh, yes! I was really, majorly angry. But a bet is a bet, and I lost. But in our Yellow Pages ad, I made sure it said 'Belle Hammermill and Cherry Pye, proprietors'."

"Was she good at running the place?" asked Betsy. "You said she brought the expertise."

"I thought she was. I know business improved, we were taking in more money every year—almost every quarter, in fact, after the first year. But our bottom line wasn't improving."

"Why not?"

"I don't know." She did an elaborate shrug. "I couldn't figure it out. Belle tried to explain it to me. Cash flow was a big problem, she said, because we were expanding our inventory. Property taxes had gone up, and of course there were two of us so profits got split in half. And there were other things. I didn't understand all of it." Cherry looked down and seemed surprised to find her hands closed into fists in her lap. She opened them to rub the palms on her thighs.

A silence fell. Jill and Betsy exchanged "are we finished?" looks, and Jill moved as if to stand, but Betsy said, "Wait a second," and she settled back again. "Cherry, is there anyone else besides Lenore who was angry with Belle?"

"I don't think so. As far as I know, the only people who really knew her here are me and Lenore."

"Do you know an Eve Suttle?"

"Why, sure! She used to work for us! But she quit and moved out of town, oh, months ago. Do you know her?"

"Not really. But she's here. She works for a shop in Savannah now."

"Savannah? That's right, that's right, she had family down there, someone told me. So she's working for a store in Savannah? Well, good for her." Cherry seemed quite pleased to hear about Eve.

"Why did she quit working for Belle? Was she fired?"

"No." Again the rolling back and forward. "It's complicated, a long story."

Jill nodded. "Tell us."

"Oh, God, it's going to make Belle sound so . . . She was a sweet person, people liked her. When we only tell the bad things, it makes her sound evil."

"Was Eve another one of Belle's people in need of help?" asked Betsy.

"Oh, gosh, yes. She was a big, fat mess, who couldn't get to work on time and who wore ugly clothes. She was an unwed mother whose kid was always sick, so she was always taking time off for the doctor, too. I thought we should fire her, but Belle said she'd help her get better. And she did. She was so nice and patient with her."

"Are you sure we're talking about the same person?" asked Betsy. "The Eve Suttle I talked to wasn't fat at all. And she was dressed very nicely."

"Was she kind of pretty? Dark red hair?" asked Cherry.

"Yes, that's her."

"Belle encouraged her to go on a diet, and dye her hair, and learn about makeup. She lost over fifty pounds and her skin cleared up when she quit eating junk food. Belle helped her get a new wardrobe and cleaned up her language, and you wouldn't believe how Eve just bloomed. And so then she got this really nice boyfriend, Jack what's his name? Something German, like Hauptman. Tall blond guy. Belle pretended that she wanted him for herself, he was so handsome. She used to flirt with him every time he came into the store. But he married Eve. And so now Belle started picking at her, in like that pattern I told you about. Where before Eve was Employee of the Month just about year-round, now she can't get through a week without being yelled at.

"And it turns out Belle wasn't just pretending to be interested in Eve's husband. The two of them really are screwing around. I think Belle was treating Eve bad because she wanted her to quit so she wouldn't find out. But Eve did find out, and there's this *huge* scene, where Eve storms in and trashes the store, throws things, breaks things. Then she goes home and kicks her husband out. Jack, it turned out, is some kind of jerk, because he moved in with Belle—and that lasted only until the divorce is final, because Belle doesn't want a jerk for a boyfriend, and anyhow now I think she lost interest as soon as Eve threw him out. It wasn't about him; it was about Eve."

"How long ago was this?"

"About six months ago, maybe more. So Eve landed on her feet, did she? That's good."

"How angry was Eve?" asked Jill.

"Angry. Damn angry. The day she came into Samplers and More and was turning over racks, Belle ran out the back because she was afraid Eve was going to attack her. Which I think she would have. She was seriously angry."

"But she got over it before she moved away," suggested Jill.

"I don't see how. Y'see, she was pregnant, and when all this happened, she lost the baby. And you don't get over that, not in a couple of months. When I heard she'd moved away, I was relieved, because she scared me when she came in that day. I was afraid she'd come back and do something like burn down the store or shoot Belle."

"Was Belle also afraid?" asked Betsy.

Cherry lifted her arms in a shrug and assumed a chipper expression, moving her head from side to side, imitating Belle. "What, me worry? No, not a bit." She dropped the pose. "I never saw Belle afraid of anything or anyone. Ever. She thought she had some kind of immunity clause on her life. Which she did, I guess. Until today."

"How angry were you at Belle?"

Cherry looked alarmed. "For what?"

"Well, for not having the expertise in running a business you thought she had."

Cherry became interested in her lap, but by now both Jill and Betsy had solid experience in waiting. At last, with a quiet sigh, Cherry said, "The shop was already established when we bought it, and so it shouldn't have gone through a long period of losing money while it built a customer base. It still isn't at the break-even point. I told Belle I wanted an independent audit after inventory in January."

Betsy asked, "Did anyone who knows you see you outside Kreinik Manufacturing's suite when Belle died?"

Belle stared at her. "Now wait just one minute!" she said. "I was mad at Belle, but I was handling it. The audit was going to tell me if things were on the up and up, okay? There was no need for me to do something stupid."

Jill said, "So humor us, were you with someone you know?"

Tightly, Cherry said, "No, I wasn't. But there were other people around, lots of people who will remember the woman in a wheelchair. I was down on the sixth floor, just like I told you. It was too crowded in the Kreinik suite to go in. But I heard Doug telling a funny story about a woman who didn't know she was insulting Kreinik Blending Filament to his face. I was just starting down the hall when I heard the scream, but I didn't go look. I went down the hall to the elevator and when I looked down from the windows in the elevator, I could see a dead woman. It was Belle." Cherry's face was pale and set, and a tear broke loose and started down her face. "This nice young man came over and bought me a brandy and talked with me until I calmed down enough to go tell someone who I was and . . . who she was." More tears spilled. "I'm sorry, I'm sorry, I can't talk anymore. Please leave."

Eighteen

Saturday, December 15, 5:05 P.M.

"Whew!" said Betsy when they left Cherry's suite. She moved her shoulders, turning her head from side to side; the tension from that interview had started a headache. "That was interesting."

"It sure puts Eve right in the crosshairs," agreed Jill. "And you saw her just one floor down from the scene of the crime. Do you want to go right from here to talk to her? I've got her room number."

"No, first let's go back to our suite," said Betsy. "We need to talk." She rubbed her forehead.

"What about?"

"What Cherry told us. Sort out the lies from the truth."

"Lies?"

"Well, one was about her being friends with Belle. First she said she was, then it became pretty clear they weren't friends at all."

"Well, I think they started out as friends, and maybe now she's dead, Cherry would like to think of her as a friend once again."

"I don't see how anyone could remain friends with someone who insults your intelligence by way of your handicap."

"Well, all right, no. But that doesn't mean she's a murderer."

"I know, I know. People put up with worse," said Betsy. "But the way her mood kept shifting . . ."

"I saw you write the word *volatile* and I agree. Made her hard to read, the way she went from pleasant to sad and then angry, all over the place. People like that make me nervous."

Betsy smiled. "Goddy's volatile," she said.

"Yes, but Goddy's fun. And not suspected of anything I could arrest him for."

"You don't like Cherry? That's funny, I kind of do."

"You can like a person without thinking they're good people," said Jill.

"True."

They went into the stairwell and started down the iron stairs. "Her reaction to your question about suicide was interesting," Betsy said, trying to speak clearly, because the depth of the hollow space, with its many hard surfaces, amplified and distorted their voices, already struggling with the echoing thunder of their feet.

"Interesting how?"

"She really liked it, jumped right on board with it."

"Well, maybe she was happy to think it was suicide rather than murder," said Jill. "Especially since you hinted that someone with a motive to murder Belle might also want to murder Cherry."

Yes, thought Betsy, deciding against continuing the conversation amid all the noise, but Jill hadn't said she thought it was murder until after Cherry eagerly agreed it might have been suicide.

They came out the door onto the eighth floor, into a carpeted silence, and turned up the hallway.

Jill said, "Do you think maybe she's not as stuck in that wheelchair as she said?"

"No, she was too specific about what she could and couldn't do. But remember how you picked Goddy up in a way that looked like what I saw with Belle? You wouldn't need to stand to grab someone by the lower legs and lift."

Jill thought about that, then nodded once. "I guess not. And she's got a lot of upper body strength."

"Yes, I noticed that. So we can't cross her off the list."

They fell silent as they turned the corner and started down toward their room on the short side. They stopped at their suite door, which was wide enough and inset deeply enough that both of them could stand between the bay windows while Betsy pulled the room key out of her name tag.

"That's clever," said Jill.

"What is, these card keys?" asked Betsy as a tiny green light on the latching mechanism lit up. She pushed the lever down to open the door.

"No, putting your room key in your badge like that."

"I forget where I learned it, but it's saved me probably a lot of hours, in total, of standing in front of a hotel or motel door trying to find the thing in my purse."

Betsy dropped her booklet onto the table and went into the bathroom. When she came out, Jill, now shoeless, was lying on the couch. "I wonder," Jill said, "if Belle did Lenore any favor by encouraging her to try selling her pattern designs."

"Well, sure she did," said Betsy. "I mean, look at the fabulous design she came up with."

"And it surprised Belle when she did, remember," said Jill.

"According to Cherry," amended Betsy. Splashing water into her eyes hadn't helped; she rubbed her left temple, where the headache seemed to be concentrating.

"All right, according to Cherry. But suppose Cherry is describing it correctly? If Belle didn't think Lenore could do it, why did she encourage Lenore to keep trying?"

"I don't know. Why?" Betsy sat down at the table and opened the seminar booklet at random.

"Because Belle was a piece of work, that's why."

"You mean a witch with a capital B?" Betsy, paging back to find her notes, paused at a list of warning signs to look for in prospective employees. One read, "Any negativity, especially in discussing people." She snorted. Sleuthing was about encouraging people to discuss the negative.

"No, I mean suppose Belle was cooking the books, stealing from Samplers and More—and cheating Cherry."

"I think Cherry suspected her, that's why she asked for that audit. That's the big motive for her. After all, that settlement has to keep her going the rest of her life." Betsy drummed her fingers on the booklet. There was something else connected to that, something Cherry said. She rubbed her forehead.

The door made a clickety sound and opened. Godwin

came in, laden with bags, in both hands and up his arms. He grinned broadly at Jill and Betsy. "What a *great* time I've had!"

"Wow, it sure looks like it!" said Betsy, flicking the switch from sleuth to shop-owner. "But wait a second, Goddy; we should look through all the stuff we've got to see if there are any—God forbid—duplicates."

"I went mostly to the floors we agreed were mine this morning," said Goddy.

"Mostly?"

"Okay, I strayed. But not far, just one floor. Did you see the beautiful crewel patterns BritStitch has?"

Betsy groaned. For a counted cross-stitch market event, the prices in BritStitch were very high. "Yes, and I bought some—did you buy some, too?"

"I thought about it, and decided to buy at least a pattern for myself, and while I was I was talking to the guy in there—he has the most *gorgeous* English accent—he noticed on my badge that I'm from Excelsior and he said someone else from that town was in there earlier today. So I told him that must be my boss from Crewel World. He says he remembered it because Excelsior is a charming name, so *very* American." Godwin pronounced it "veddy" and assumed a lofty air, in imitation of the man, whom Betsy remembered as charming and not at all supercilious.

She said, "God bless my hometown forever, since it kept you from spending money on patterns I've already bought. But if you were in BritStitch, I assume you were in other suites on that floor?"

With a comic effort, Godwin raised his right arm and its burden of purchases to swear, "On my honor, boss, BritStitch was the first place I went into on six. I couldn't resist that one of the sheep in front of the stone fence, but I paid for it out of my own pocket, since it's going to be mine. It's beautiful!"

"I know, I bought one for myself and two more for the shop. But if you, Mr. Needlepoint, like it, maybe we should buy another one or two tomorrow. Meanwhile, come on," said Betsy, leading the way. "Let's see what you've got."

They went through the short hallway into the bedroom. A great drift of white plastic bags was piled against the wall under the window.

"My word, you have been busy!" she said.

Jill came in behind them. "Say, before you get started, how about some dinner? My stomach thinks my throat's been cut. Or are you two all right? I can go down alone."

Godwin, piling his newest purchases on the floor, said, "I could eat something. A cow, a pig, a horse, even a dog. Cooked or raw, I'm not fussy."

Betsy started to disagree, then realized that headache she'd been trying to ignore was from hunger. "All right," she said. "Food first, inventory later." But her eye was caught by lights beyond the thin curtains at the window, and she went there first to look out. Down at the bottom of the hill, the lights from other motels were showing clearly. "Hey, it's stopped snowing! And see, up there! A star."

"Great!" cheered Godwin, coming for a look. "We can start moving some of this stuff out to the trailer."

"Better ask at the desk if they'll loan you a shovel," said Jill. "They don't do snow plowing here, remember?"

"Maybe the snow will remember this is the South and melt away overnight," said Betsy.

"Incurable optimist," sighed Godwin to Jill. "I've tried

and I've tried, but she just doesn't understand that the world's a frying pan and we're all eggs."

They took the elevator down to the atrium floor and after one look at the line waiting at the restaurant, joined the mob packed into the bar.

The bar was out of hamburgers and hot dogs—a notice to that effect was posted on a white board propped over the cash register. They had one kind of soup left: tomato. There were sandwiches: salami and cheese, cheese and tomato, and pimento and cheese, all on white bread. "The *delivery trucks!* Can't! Get! Here!" the bartender bawled over the din, jabbing a forefinger downward.

Jill nodded in comprehension and held up three fingers. "Beer!" she shouted. "Tomato soup! Three of each!"

"Wow," she said awhile later, working her way out of the bar with a tray and heading for the elevators. Godwin and Betsy waited there for her. "This is about all I could get, unless one of you would prefer a pimento and cheese sandwich on white bread."

"Gah," said Betsy.

"Wait a second," said Godwin, and he sprinted across the atrium to a tiny shop next to the lobby entrance. He came back with a bag of corn chips and two outsize PayDay candy bars. "This about cleans them out, too," he said glumly. "I hate to think what we'll be having for breakfast in the morning."

They took the tray up to their suite, and sat down at the round table to eat. Jill brewed a fresh pot of coffee, but she was the only one who drank any.

"All right," said Godwin, scattering corn chips over his soup, "what did you two find out from Cherry Pye?"

"That Belle wasn't a nice person," replied Betsy, taking the bag of corn chips he handed her and imitating his scatter over her own soup.

"So Cherry says, anyway," said Jill, reaching for the chips.

"Is Cherry a suspect, then?" asked Godwin.

"Don't you think she should be?"

"No." Godwin shook his head. "If she hated Belle enough to murder her, why would she be almost hysterical over her death?"

Jill said, "Betsy and I were talking about that. A lot of cops can tell you stories of men who call 911, crying and everything, to say they just shot someone. They get mad, and run over, hit or shoot whoever they're mad at, then the adrenaline drains off and they're scared and sorry."

Godwin smiled and said, "But these are women."

Jill said, "I have a friend who's a toxicologist, worked for a poison center for awhile. She once told me that while almost everyone in prison for murder is male, she doesn't think the sexes are all that different. Women don't get that testosterone rush, but they are just as capable of hatred as men."

Godwin smiled. "And they reach for the poison bottle, don't they? And they aren't sorry later."

"Still, it seems that in the case of all three of our suspects there was a long-term buildup of hatred. Betsy thinks this murder was an impulsive thing. Belle was at the railing and it was easy to walk over, lift and let go," Jill said.

Betsy said, "It almost doesn't matter who murdered Belle; the release is because she's dead, not because the person crying murdered her."

"I bet one of them is crying because she murdered Belle," argued Godwin.

"Godwin's right about the poison, however," Jill said "It's a shame she didn't do what angry women traditionally do, put poison in her food."

"Why would you prefer our murderer used poison?" asked Betsy.

"Because then we probably wouldn't know anything about it. It's not hard to get hold of, and with a little bit of care, it's one of the safest methods. It's what I'd use."

Godwin stared at Jill. "You have depths I never knew about," he said.

Jill smiled at him. "I couldn't ever get mad enough at you to poison you, Goddy. But if you annoyed me enough, I'd start giving you tickets. Parking tickets and speeding tickets and littering tickets and operating an unsafe motor vehicle tickets—"

"Enough, enough!" cried the young man. "Betsy, if ever our inventory lists don't balance out, it's because I'm bribing a police officer with all the Kreinik gold braid she wants!" He looked back at Jill. "Are you going to eat those last three corn chips?"

They ate everything, even the PayDay candy bars.

Then Godwin and Betsy retired to the bedroom to go over their purchases. Jill turned on the Weather Channel and found that temperatures were to remain below normal until Sunday afternoon, when they would at last rise into the forties.

She changed channels and found the really good *Christmas Carol* movie, the one with Alistair Sim, got out the Santa pin and strung some more beads. The project worked up quickly, she was nearly done when Godwin and Betsy came back into the sitting room.

"Now what?" asked Jill, shutting off the television.

"There's a pajama party downstairs," hinted Godwin.

"No, we have more questions to ask, I think," said Betsy. "What time is it?"

Jill checked her watch. "Eight forty-seven. Not too late to go talk to Eve Suttle. That's her name, not Saddle but Suttle."

"She's the one you found sitting on the floor and crying, right?" Godwin asked Betsy.

"Yes." Betsy frowned, trying to recall the details of the encounter. "She said Belle helped her get her life together and was very nice to her. At first, anyway. Those are the words she used, 'at first.' Then something happened—she didn't say what—and she moved back to Savannah to be with family."

"Cherry said it was because Belle took her husband away from her," Jill noted.

"Do you think that could be true?" asked Godwin, amazed at Belle's wickedness.

"Not only that," said Betsy, "the stress of it caused Eve to abort her pregnancy."

"Oh, my God!" said Godwin. "But wait, wait, didn't you say before that she has a little girl?"

"That's from a different pregnancy. She was a single mother when she first came to work for Belle and Cherry. A real mess, according to Cherry. Belle was very supportive and helpful until Eve became an attractive woman who was courted by and married a handsome man, at which point Belle turned on her."

"All of this according to Cherry," Jill pointed out.

A little silence fell. Godwin said, "Maybe you've got it all wrong. Maybe it's Cherry. Cherry hid the note to Belle about getting Lenore's model done earlier; Cherry seduced

Eve's husband; Cherry was running the shop into the ground; it's all Cherry. And Belle was going to reveal her wickednesses—is that a word, wickednesses?—so Cherry had to kill her."

Before Betsy could think up a reply to that, the phone rang. She went to answer it, and a man's jolly voice said, "Are you the one trying to find eyewitnesses to that accident this morning?"

"Yes, why?"

"Because I think we have some information for you. This is Frank Bialec. Judy and I are in Room 834. Judy has some information about that terrible thing that happened this morning. Can you come over here?"

"I suppose so, yes."

"We'd come to you but we're feeding the sugar gliders." He said to someone in his room, "What? I'll be right there, I'm on the phone." And to Betsy, "Thanks, I'll see you in a little while." And he hung up.

Betsy hung up and tried to rerun that strange sentence. Maybe she'd hadn't heard him right. "We'd come to you but we're feeding the sugar gliders." Nothing sensible she could think of sounded like "feeding the sugar gliders." She turned to Jill and Godwin and said, "Is 'sugar gliders' a new slang term for moochers?"

Godwin stared at her. "Not that I know of. Sugar gliders: Sounds like hummingbirds on ice skates. Who's got sugar gliders?"

"Frank and Judy Bialic. Do you know them?"

Godwin said, "Sure, and so do you. He and his wife are Mosey 'n Me."

"Oh, the designers!" said Betsy. "I don't think I've ever

heard their last names before." Mosey 'n Me published fun and easy counted cross-stitch patterns of amusing, cartoon-like bears, Santas, and homemade-looking charts of stars to be stitched in muted or dusty primary colors.

"*And* he is one of those people who helps amateur painters and carpenters on that TV show *Trading Spaces*," said Jill.

Betsy felt her stomach go cold as she demanded, "Did one of you volunteer my apartment for a surprise makeover?"

"No," they said hastily, and "Of course not!"

"Good," said Betsy. "Because if either of you ever, ever lets someone come in to mess with *my* bedroom or kitchen, I'll come and paint *your* bedroom or kitchen with tar and feathers!"

Jill hid a smile poorly. "Sounds like someone saw the episode that made the woman cry."

Godwin asked frankly, "What makes you think we'd do something like that?"

"Because he wants to talk to us. Frank does." Betsy rubbed the place on her temple where the headache used to be. Was it coming back? "They'd come over here, except they're 'feeding the sugar gliders'."

Jill said, "It's a little furry animal from Australia."

Betsy looked sideways at her, not sure if she was serious. "Who is?"

But Jill said, "Sugar gliders. They have the sweetest little faces. For awhile they were the latest thing in pets, after African pygmy hedgehogs and before prairie dogs."

"How come you know about them and I don't?"

"Because between tracking down murderers and running your own business, you don't have time to pay attention to exotic pet fads."

"Well, he did say something about you asking for eyewitnesses to Belle's fall. Maybe that's what they want to talk to us about, the murder of Belle Hammermill."

Godwin said, "Can I come along? Not to hear the information, I want to see the sugar gliders. They sound too sweet."

Nineteen

Frank Bialec was a short, stocky man with white hair and beard, both cropped close around an extraordinarily likable face set with warm blue eyes. The living room portion of his suite was full of stock and the paraphernalia of a teacher: easel with big white tablet, handouts, and stitchery kits. He was wearing red jeans, red suspenders, and red high-top shoes. Judy was not in sight, but the door to the bedroom was closed.

"I'm Betsy Devonshire, this is Jill Cross Larson, and this is Godwin DuLac," said Betsy. "You called?"

"Yes, yes, come in, come in!" said Frank with a big smile

that abruptly faded as he went on, "Actually, it's my wife you want to speak to. The one of you that's a police detective."

"Well," said Jill, "half of that would be me, and the other half is Ms. Devonshire. I'm only a desk sergeant; Betsy is the sleuth."

Godwin said, "I work for Betsy, I'm Vice President in Charge of Operations at Crewel World, Incorporated, and Editor in Chief of *Hasta la Stitches,* our newsletter." Godwin loved to give his full title. "But I really came because I want to see the sugar gliders."

Frank said, "There are no sugar gliders here, the hotel doesn't allow pets." He raised his eyebrows, nodded significantly, then winked. "Okay?"

"You mean you have more than one?" asked Godwin.

"Do you see any sugar gliders around here, son?" said Frank, at the same time nodding in the affirmative.

"How many don't you have?" asked Betsy.

"An even dozen."

Godwin whistled.

"I'll take you back one at a time," said Frank. "They get excited when they see too many strangers at once."

Betsy, because she had another, more important, reason to speak with Judy, went first.

She found a slim, attractive woman with silver-and-iron hair standing between two stacks of hamster cages in various sizes. She was wearing an apron over a blue turtleneck sweater and slicing a banana into a bowl. "Excuse me if I keep on working. They have to be fed several times a day, and they just love fresh fruit," she said. "I'm Judy Bialec."

"Hi, I'm Betsy Devonshire. Your husband said you wanted to talk to me?"

"About—?" said Judy.

"The death of Belle Hammermill."

The slicing stopped. "Oh! I'm sorry, I thought you were a shop-owner."

Betsy smiled. "I am. And I carry your Mosey 'n Me patterns. I'm sorry we arrived too late for your class yesterday. Several people told me the two of you are a riot."

Judy smiled and finished slicing the banana as she said, "Well . . . not a riot, not really. But we do our best to amuse as well as instruct." Judy took the bowl and went to one stack of cages. Betsy turned to peer over her shoulder.

"Want to see one?"

"May I?"

Judy opened a cage and reached in. She turned and enclosed in her fist was a small, pale-gray creature with black stripes running up its wide flat head. Its ears were oversized and round, its black eyes were enormous, and its pink nose wiggled. It looked like the most charming alien Industrial Light and Magic could invent.

"May I touch it?" Betsy asked softly.

"Certainly."

Betsy stroked the tiny head with a forefinger, and found the fur delightfully soft. The sugar glider made a high-pitched inquiring sound, and twisted in Judy's hand, trying to sniff her finger.

"This is Mama, our senior sugar glider, boss of this pack." Judy indicated the stack of cages from which Mama had come. "We have enough of them that they have divided into two tribes."

"Are you breeding them?" asked Betsy.

"No. We're rescuing them. People buy them without realizing how much trouble they are."

"How can something this small be trouble?" asked Betsy, amused, stroking again.

"To stay healthy they must eat only fresh food. Fresh fruit, fresh vegetables, live mealworms, fresh chicken, four times a day. Nothing canned, nothing preserved, nothing leftover even from earlier in the day. And clean, pure water. They must be kept warm and out of drafts. And you can't have just one, unless you give it constant attention, because they are tribal creatures and need at least one close friend. Fail in any of this, and they get sick, and, too often, they die. To me, the main thing wrong with them is that they are so adorable that people see them and want them and buy them without doing any research. When they realize how much trouble sugar glider are, they throw them away. Sometimes I get to them before they die."

"Poor babies, don't know how lucky they are to have you, I bet. They're from Australia, is that right?"

"Yes," said Judy, putting Mama back into her cage.

"Are they marsupials?"

"Yes. They also have that flap of skin between their front and back legs like flying squirrels, and can glide like them. In the wild they lap sweet sap from trees. That's why they're called sugar gliders."

"Huge eyes," Betsy said, "so nocturnal?"

"Sort of. They're active mostly in the early morning and late evening. That's called *crepuscular.*"

Betsy snorted. "It sounds like a skin disease."

Judy picked up the bowl of bananas and went to the other stack of cages. "I haven't fed this bunch yet." She opened a cage and reached in with some slices of bananas in her fingers and yanked her hand back as the cage erupted with tiny

growls and miniature squeals and the sound of small creatures rushing about.

"Oops, I forgot to wash my hand. Did I mention that my
two tribes are at war? This tribe *hates* Mama, even the smell
of her."

Judy went to wash, and the helium-fueled threats of may-
hem gradually subsided. Betsy, peering into the cages to see
them busy grooming ruffled fur back into place, didn't know
whether she was amused or dismayed by this display of envy
and hatred among these darling, elfin creatures.

When Judy came back and after she had fed her charges,
Betsy said, "You had something to tell me about Belle
Hammermill's death."

Judy's face turned solemn. "I don't know if it's important, but Frank said I should let you decide."

"What is it?"

"I came up here this morning around ten to give my
gliders their midmorning snack, and I came out just in time
to hear that awful scream as the woman fell. I couldn't believe it, and I looked up to see where she had fallen from.
The strands of ivy on the ninth floor were waving, so I assumed that's where she started from."

"Did you see anyone else up there?" asked Betsy.

"No. At least, I don't think so. But there was some kind
of movement. I . . . can't describe it, exactly. It was as if
someone wearing something dark and sparkly was crawling
on her hands and knees."

Betsy could only stare at Judy, her mind working that
one over.

"I know, isn't that the oddest thing? But that's what I
thought it was. Or—you know how people will put a T-shirt
on a Lab? Maybe that's what it was. I mean, I got my sugar

gliders into the hotel, maybe someone else brought a dog. And then put a sparkly shirt on it and sent it trotting down the gallery. Only I think, before it got to the corner it went into a room."

"Did you see a door open and close?"

"No, but I wasn't at an angle where I could see the doors. All I can tell you is that there was a twinkle, it moved, and then it was gone. I'm not sure when it went away, because I couldn't see very well, there are those flower boxes, and the banisters. So it was glimpses of fragments, y'know? But it seemed to go away before it got to the end of the gallery."

"Might it have just gone back along the wall? I got a lesson earlier today in how things vanish if they step back from the railing."

Judy thought about that. "All right, that might be what happened."

"Which means whatever it was could have gone down to the corner and around it."

"Yes."

Betsy thought for a bit. "Could it have been someone in a wheelchair?" That made more sense, the wheels turning, seen through the balusters.

It was Judy's turn to try to picture this. "Well . . . yes, I suppose so. Hmmm . . . yes, that makes sense to me. Though wait a second, you'd think I'd see more of the chair, wouldn't you? And the person in it. But I didn't."

Betsy thought some more. "Please don't be insulted, but how sure are you that you really saw something?"

"Oh, I really saw something. We have a lot of animals at home, and I'm quick to spot movement, especially sneaky movement." Judy frowned in thought. "It wasn't something small, like a ball or a cat, but large, like a big dog or a child.

It wasn't tall—like a person walking—it was low, and dark, and somehow there was a twinkle or sparkle, and it was moving fast."

"Which way?"

"To the left." Judy raised a forefinger to a little above eye level and moved it a few inches. "That's all. I'm sorry, I guess that isn't very helpful."

That was true, but it was something peculiar, and on the scene, so who knew? She said, "I don't know what is or isn't helpful. And even if it isn't, I got to meet these beautiful sugar gliders."

"Would you consider acquiring one as a pet?"

"Sorry, no."

"Good girl."

Betsy went back out into the sitting room. "Oh, Goddy, they are just the prettiest little things!"

"Good, me next!" announced Godwin, and he slipped past her into the bedroom.

Jill and Betsy were invited to find places on the sofa, and they did. "May I get you something to drink? We have Seven-Up, Coke, and mineral water."

"Coke, please," said Jill.

"Water, thank you," said Betsy.

Jill asked Betsy, "What did she tell you?"

Betsy told her about the "sparkly" sighting.

Jill thought that over while Frank brought them their drinks. "What do you think?" she said at last.

"I have no idea," said Betsy. "Frank, what did you think when she told you?"

"That she saw something real. I'm the one with the weird imagination." He sat in an upholstered chair and put one red-canvased ankle on his knee. "But what it might have been, I don't know. Who goes crawling around on the floor carrying sparklers?"

"Beats me," said Jill.

"Still," said Frank, "we decided that since you are taking an interest in what might have happened, you should hear about this. What do you think? Is it a real clue?"

"I'm not sure," said Betsy. "Maybe not, since what she saw was probably not a person."

"But what else could it be?" he asked.

"I have no idea."

The talk turned to the world of needlework design, which lasted until Godwin came out. "I want one," he announced.

"No, you don't," said Betsy.

"Yes, I do, I really do. But I won't get one because in about three weeks I'd start looking for short cuts in feeding, and they'd get sick and I'd feel guilty. Still, those three weeks would be really sweet. Do you know she takes them on airplanes and everything? Just sticks them in her pockets and down the front of her shirt and no one knows a thing."

"So much for airline security," noted Jill.

The door to the bedroom opened and Judy came out. She looked a little surprised to find three guests instead of two.

Frank said, "Sergeant Cross, do you have anything to ask Judy?"

"Just one thing," Jill replied. "I haven't got Betsy's wild-card talent for investigations, and I haven't had department training as an investigator. But I did wonder—" she turned to Judy "—How fast was this sparkly thing moving?"

"About as fast as a yellow Lab can trot," Judy replied. "Or so it seemed to me."

"Thank you."

Godwin said, "Jill, go take a look at those sugar gliders, you'll just fall in love."

"No, I don't think so," said Jill. "I have a weakness for soft, furry things, but I have someone to love and take care of already." She put her empty glass on the end table and said, "It's getting late, we should let these people rest up for tomorrow."

Betsy stood and said, "Thank you so much for calling us about this. What Judy told me is certainly intriguing."

As the trio went back up the gallery toward their room, Betsy told Godwin what Judy said she'd seen that morning.

"Sounds like the sort of clue that not even Miss Marple would get," he said. "Do you know what it means?"

"No."

"Well, maybe it's nothing; maybe it's not important."

"No, no, I think it is important," said Betsy. "This is the first eyewitness account that someone might've really been up there. And . . ."

"And?"

"Something . . . I don't know. It's like someone at the very back of a big crowd, waving his hand to get my attention. Hard to tell."

Jill looked at her askance. "You're a strange one."

"Look who's talking, Miss Let's-Throw-Goddy-Over-A-Rail."

"I never let go of him, never."

"True," said Godwin. "Even when I wriggled and said, 'O my *dear*!' " He hurried out ahead of them and did a little waggle as he walked on, looking over his shoulder with eyebrows lifted and his mouth in a shocked O.

"Are you hiding a sugar glider in there, or do you need a

dose of that itch cream you carry in your suitcase?" asked Jill.

"Ooo-ooo, made you mad, made you mad."

"Stop it, both of you," said Betsy, laughing.

Back in their suite, Jill asked, "Do you want me to call Eve Suttle or Lenore King to see if they'll talk to you this evening?"

Betsy checked her watch. It was barely nine-thirty, but she was tired. It had been a late night last night, and a long day today. "I don't think I could ask an intelligent question, or understand the answer if I could," she said. "Let's do it to-morrow. I want to go to bed."

But lying in bed soon after, she couldn't fall asleep. She thought about getting up and doing some needlework, but that might disturb Jill. And Godwin was asleep in the sitting room, so she couldn't go there, either. She slipped out of bed, found her copy of the Management and Hiring booklet— her choices were that or the Gideon Bible, and somehow she didn't feel up to King James's English—and went into the bathroom. The regular light switch, she knew, also turned on a roaring exhaust fan, so she twisted the timer on an overhead heating light, and sat down to read.

She found a list of "red lights" to look for while inter-viewing a prospective employee—she'd had two bad experi-ences this year with employees who'd left after a few weeks—and decided that the red lights both employees had shown was lack of enthusiasm and lack of chemistry. She was about to turn the page and explore the positive signs to look for, when her eye was caught by the notes she'd made while interviewing Cherry Pye.

It had been a long interview. Betsy's notes covered three pages. She noted with a wry smile her first note: *volatile.* Too true. On the other hand, Cherry had seemed convincingly reluctant to put others in a bad light. And her story about Lenore's model jibed with Lenore's own account of Belle's misbehavior. Interesting that both Lenore and Eve ran into the same strange jealousy problem with Belle.

Had Cherry?

Betsy ran her eyes back over the notes. The money to buy the store was Cherry's. Belle supplied "the expertise," according to Cherry. Cherry said the shop was owned fifty-fifty, but it if was losing money, it was losing *Cherry's* money.

Could Cherry afford that?

The light went out. Betsy stood and groped for the dial, found and twisted it, and sat down again to read some more.

Cherry said Belle had explained the reasons for the losses to her: cash flow problems, an increase in inventory, having to split the profits. And if Cherry had asked for an audit, that meant she suspected Belle was lying.

So there was a motive—no. Betsy was starting to get sleepy now, so had to think it out slowly. If Belle was stealing money from Samplers and More, and Cherry was threatening an audit that would reveal it, then the person who should have gone over the railing was Cherry, not Belle. Right?

Betsy sighed, closed the booklet, turned out the light, and went to bed.

Twenty

Sunday, December 16, 7:56 A.M.

Betsy was wakened the next morning by the sound of voices whispering. She understood at once the whisperers were benign because she came awake hearing, ". . . going to wear my lavender shirt, but maybe that's a little frivolous, and anyway I think this tan looks just as good with the black sport coat, don't you think?"

Godwin. In her bedroom? No, this was not her bed, so not her bedroom. Where—?

Oh, Nashville. Market. Blizzard. Murder—oh, have mercy! Murder! She sighed.

The owner of the other voice spoke aloud, "Betsy, are you awake?"

Jill.

Betsy was sure there was an implied "at last" in there somewhere. "Uh-huh," she murmured. "Wha' timesit?"

"Nearly eight."

"Uff."

"We're thinking we need to get down to breakfast pretty soon because who knows what they'll have to eat, and the best of it will soon be gone."

Remembering the Fritos scattered on her tomato soup last night, Betsy sighed again and began to struggle out of bed.

But once up, she was washed and dressed in a very efficient hurry. She came out into the sitting room in her brand new cranberry sweater and navy skirt, and Godwin said admiringly, "How do you do that?"

"I pretend I'm back in boot camp," said Betsy. "It might've been a long time ago, but something you learn in an advanced state of terror never quite leaves you."

"Terror?" Godwin was leading the way to the door. "I thought you were in the Navy, not the Marine Corps."

"I was in the Navy, but when you're eighteen years old and people are shouting and blowing whistles at five A.M. and insisting you hit the line, now, at attention, bare feet at a forty-five degree angle, middle finger lined up with the side seams of your nightgown—and you do—you realize that when you're really scared you can do anything required of you. Even take a shower and get dressed in eight minutes. It was a surreal experience, one I'm glad I signed up for, but never, ever want to try again."

Jill snickered.

"What?" asked Betsy, falling behind Godwin, who was practically cantering down the gallery toward the elevators. Breakfast smells of meat and biscuits were wafting all the way to them from down on the atrium floor.

"I had a great-aunt who was a Navy WAVE, and you sound just like her. She wouldn't have missed it for anything, but never wanted to go back."

The elevator came half full of people from the ninth floor, and stopped to pick up a few more from seven. Most were in that early-morning daze that wants neither to talk nor listen. Someone did murmur something about the hotel extending breakfast hours to ease crowding, but no one replied.

As the car smoothly descended, Betsy turned and looked out at the rising view. "Hey," she said, "is that Cherry?"

Jill managed to turn around in the small, crowded space and look out in time to see someone moving down the gallery right across from them. She was in a wheelchair, moving swiftly toward the elevators on that side.

"Where?" asked Godwin, wriggling around to peer out.

"Up there," said Jill, pointing. "But it's not Cherry, her hair's the wrong color." The person she was looking at had very pale, perhaps white, hair.

The balusters of the metal railing, and the ivy dripping from the flower boxes, broke her image up so that for Godwin she was more a flicker than an image going by. Jill and Betsy exchanged significant looks. "What good eyes, you two have," Godwin said. He was a bit nearsighted, but this was as close as he could come to admitting it.

Breakfast wasn't so awful as Betsy expected. No fresh melon or strawberries, no croissants or sweet rolls, no bread or English muffins to toast—but there were plenty of biscuits and enough butter or jam for them. There were bacon and sausages, and pancakes with syrup. The kitchen was out of eggs, except for the few stirred into a mix of fried potatoes with add-ons of onion and sweet bell peppers. More biscuits waited to have sausage gravy or a ham and cheese sauce spooned over them. There was coffee and tea, but no milk. The little bin that had held tiny half-and-half containers was empty. There was cranberry juice, but no orange or grapefruit juice. Betsy got the last orange. She peeled it and shared the sections with Godwin and Jill. Before long, they were lingering over the last of the coffee—the place wasn't nearly as jammed as last night, so they were in no hurry to leave the table—and talking about plans for the day.

"I don't see Eve Suttle or Lenore King here," said Jill, craning her neck.

"May I join you?" asked a slim woman with white hair combed into a smooth helmet. She was in a wheelchair, and Betsy suddenly recognized her as the INRG Committee member behind the table in the lobby from yesterday. She had a tray in her lap bearing a cup of coffee and a single biscuit.

"Yes, please," said Betsy, and Godwin hastily pulled an empty chair away to make room for her.

"We're about finished," said Jill. "Do you have someone else who will sit with you?"

"No, but I cherish a few minutes alone at breakfast," said the woman, transferring the tray to the table. "I'm Emily Watson, co-chair of this event."

Betsy introduced herself, Jill and Godwin.

"You're the one who brought her to this event," said Emily to Betsy, nodding at Jill. "We issued your friend a special name tag so she could buy something to keep her occupied.

But you found something else to do," she said to Jill. "Trying to find out what really happened to Belle Hammermill. I am sure you will find it was sad accident or, at worst, a suicide. And that's why I came to your table—to beg you not to do anything more to disrupt this event than you absolutely have to. Ms. Harrison, who is normally just the night manager, is de facto day manager as well; and she is, quite naturally, upset about what happened yesterday morning. She is anxious that whatever needs to be done, be done quietly and without disturbing the guests. She spoke rather sharply to me this morning about your, er, methods."

"Yes, she has spoken to us, as well," Jill said. "I am going to tell you something in strict confidence."

Jill paused while Emily studied her face and then nodded. "All right," she said.

"We are trying to solve what we are now convinced is a murder."

Emily gasped and stared at the three of them, who returned the look solemnly.

"I see," she said. "Then why—? I mean, I'm sorry, but it seems from the descriptions I've heard of your antics around the upper-floor railings that you are amusing yourselves, rather than conducting a serious investigation."

"We are taking it very seriously," said Jill. "Those two experiments at the railings were important, and they served the purpose of convincing us that Ms. Hammermill did not go over by accident or by her own will. And having served that purpose, they won't be repeated."

"I am glad to hear that," Emily said. "But I am terribly shocked to think you actually believe someone might have pushed Ms. Hammermill to her death. I trust the reason was such that we need have no fear of it happening again?"

"I doubt that very much," said Betsy.

"Good." Emily looked relieved, broke her biscuit and said, "So this was a terrible thing, but an isolated thing. I don't want people's noses ground into it, or they might begin to feel they can't come to the Market in the future without being sickened or terrified."

"I understand," said Betsy quietly.

Emily put a dab of preserves on a fragment of biscuit. "I feel especially sorry for Cherry Pye, Ms. Hammermill's partner in business."

Betsy nodded. "Yes, Jill and I spoke with her yesterday afternoon, but she doesn't seem to be here for breakfast."

"I understand that she has elected to stay in her room until she can leave the hotel," Emily said. "So it's not because she's in danger?"

"I don't think so," said Betsy.

"Then I'm sorry she's elected to isolate herself. It was good to have another woman on display who is both a paraplegic and a success in business."

Betsy asked, "Are you and she the only two?"

"In INRG? Oh no, there are others. But not many; it takes a certain degree of courage and effort to succeed in business when you're confined to a wheelchair."

"Do you know Cherry?" asked Jill.

"Not well. She only joined INRG a few years ago. She's especially brave. She jumped right into owning a store; she hadn't worked in retail at all before."

"She told us that Belle brought the expertise to the business."

"Yes, I'd heard that, too."

"There are probably all kinds of special problems when

you're in a wheelchair if you decide to go into the retail business," said Betsy.

"Oh, goodness, yes!" Emily seemed amused that Betsy should say something so obvious. "If you work in the store, and of course you have to if you want to make any money, all the aisles must be wide enough for your chair, which cuts into display space. And you have to have someone always in the store with you, because you can't reach up high, and there's always that individual who thinks that having a spinal injury means your IQ is about forty points lower than average, which can be enraging when she's the fourteenth customer that day who speaks very. Slowly. And. Clearly."

Betsy chuckled. "At least it's not like a lot of other retail businesses, where they only want to talk to the man, even if he's brand new that day."

"That's right," agreed Emily.

"It must be expensive," noted Jill, "having to rework the aisles—and make the doorways wider and have the sills flattened."

"Yes. And you have to stick to your diet, because extra-wide chairs call for even wider aisles." She chuckled. "Not that even the narrow chairs aren't always nicking the counters and door frames. But the worst is dropping things. I finally had a special attachment put on my chair so I didn't have to carry my long-reach in one hand all day long."

"Long reach?" asked Godwin, pausing in the act of cutting another bite from his pancakes.

"You know, that tool that extends your reach." She lifted her right hand up near her shoulder and moved the fingers as if pulling a trigger, while at the same time extending her left arm to move the fingers as if pinching something. "So you can pick things up from the floor or from a high shelf."

"Oh, a grabber." Godwin nodded. Jill leaned a little sideways to look at Emily's chair for the attachment.

"It's on the chair I use in my shop," she said. "This is my outing chair, with arms and a place to attach a basket for my purchases." She turned her face to Betsy and said in a tone almost pleading, "I really don't understand how you can think this was no accident."

"I'm afraid Jill and I both do," said Betsy.

"So then, you must suspect . . . someone?"

"Not yet."

"Which one of you is the policeman?" She was looking at Godwin.

"I am," said Jill.

"Ha!" she exclaimed. "Making the same mistake I hate for others to make!"

"That's all right," said Godwin, very amused. "I didn't mind."

Emily said to Jill, "I apologize. Now that I look at you, I believe I remember seeing you go into the hotel office to speak with that police investigator yesterday."

"Yes, that was me."

"Did he say you could conduct your own investigation?"

"Yes, provided I passed along anything we found out to him. His name is Lieutenant Paul Birdsong."

Emily nodded. "An easy name to remember. Do you think you will be able to discover the, er, perpetrator of this unfortunate occurrence?"

The trio looked at one another. Godwin said, "Yes, I'm sure they will." When Emily looked quizzically at him, he said, "I'm Ms. Devonshire's Vice President in Charge of Operations at Crewel World, *and* Editor in Chief of our newsletter. I'm doing the buying while Betsy is sleuthing."

Emily's slim-penciled eyebrows rose. "I thought Sergeant Larson was conducting the investigation."

"We're working together," said Jill. "Ms. Devonshire has proved herself very competent in criminal investigations. She has a natural talent for it, for which our department back home has been grateful on previous occasions."

"Really." The trio nodded, so Emily, with a slight shake of her head, broke another fragment off her biscuit and said, "Very well."

Betsy asked impulsively, "Were you on the third or fourth floor a little while ago?"

"Why yes, I was on four. Why do you ask?"

"Because we thought we saw someone in a wheelchair."

"It was me. I had to deliver a message to someone."

Godwin said, "Is this the first year there's been snow in Nashville during the Market?"

"Oh, no, we've had snow before. Just not so much. It really is an emergency for the city right now. I understand there are power outages in some districts; we're fortunate not to have that to cope with as well. I don't suppose you find it so difficult when it snows back home as we find it here."

Godwin launched into some Minnesota blizzard stories, which Betsy tuned out. She was thinking of something . . .

"Betsy?" It was Jill.

"Hmm?"

"Come on, we're leaving."

"What?"

"Aren't you coming?" Betsy looked up and saw Jill and Godwin standing.

"Oh. Sure, I guess so. We'll let the committee know if there are any developments, Ms. Watson."

"Thank you."

Betsy remained in a withdrawn state as they made their way back to the elevators. "What are you thinking about?" Jill finally asked as they got off on their floor.

"Did you see the way those wheels twinkled on her wheelchair?"

Godwin said, "What, does she have Christmas lights on them? Darn, I missed that!"

"No, no, I mean when she was wheeling down that gallery, when we saw her from the elevator."

Jill shook her head at Betsy. "Cherry's wheelchair has thick plastic spokes."

Betsy stopped and closed her eyes, summoning the image of Cherry in her suite. Her wheelchair had been an armless variety with thin canvas seat and back, quite different from the sturdier kind Emily sat in. "Yes, that's right." She sighed, another theory gone west.

"Are you going to go shopping today?" asked Godwin.

Betsy carded open the door to their suite. "No, I guess not. So Goddy, be sure to see Cross-Stitch Wonders on two today. There are a lot of fans of their Northwest patterns. And Dragon Dreaams is on two as well, I think. I want to be sure to bring back some of their dragon patterns."

"There's a row of four or five suites that feature fantasy charts," said Godwin. "Some of the people in there are wearing medieval costumes."

Jill made a face, but Betsy said to Godwin, "There is a little subculture of young women who really like that kind of thing, so be sure to visit them all."

"Gotcha."

Godwin gathered his Market listing, made sure he had the credit card, and left.

"Well, it seemed like a good idea for a moment there," grumbled Betsy. "Didn't you notice the way the wheels on her chair glittered between the balusters when we were coming down on the elevator? Damn."

"Is it ever that easy?" asked Jill. "So back to the slog. Let's see who's available to talk to next, Eve or Lenore."

Jill called Eve and found her in her room and prepared to talk "if it's for not too long—Mrs. Entwhistle gave me another list."

They took the stairs down a floor, and knocked on Eve's door.

The door was opened by a very tall, thin woman with dark, hooded eyes and a high, narrow nose. "May I help you?" she asked. She had a decided southern accent, but there was a lot more steel than magnolia about her.

"We're here to talk with Eve Suttle," said Jill, using her crispest tone and steadiest stare.

The thin woman blinked first. "Very well," she said, and stepped back so Jill and Betsy could come in. "Eve?" she called. "Those two people you told me about are here to talk to you."

"Yes, ma'am!" came a voice from the bedroom.

The door to the inner room opened and a strikingly attractive young woman with auburn curls and large, light-brown eyes came out. She was wearing a cream-colored blouse with a wide collar in some silky material and a split skirt that very nearly matched the mahogany of her hair. The only incongruous note was the clear plastic envelope slung around her neck on a white elastic cord. It contained a card on which was printed in large black letters: *Eve Suttle, Savannah, GA*.

She smiled when she saw Betsy. "I remember you!" she said. "You were the woman who was so kind to me yesterday morning! I don't think I ever thanked you for bringing me back here to my room." She held out her hand.

Betsy took it. "I was glad to help. And I want to thank you for agreeing to talk to us now." Betsy turned to the tall, thin woman. "You must be Mrs. Entwhistle. I'm so glad you can spare Eve for this interview. It won't take long."

"Hmph," said Mrs. Entwhistle. "I'll be on five, Eve. You have your list for three. We'll meet back here at noon." She turned and walked out of the suite, closing the door with just the slightest hint of emphasis.

"Is she very upset with you?" asked Betsy.

"She'll get over it. This terrible thing that happened to Belle has everyone on edge."

"Then perhaps she understands how necessary this interview is. Won't you sit down?" Betsy moved to the round table under its swag light.

She and Jill waited until Eve was comfortably seated before sitting themselves, flanking her. Betsy opened the Management and Hiring book. Eve, seeing it, said, "Did you go to Betsy Stinner's class?"

"No, we got here too late. Did you?"

"No, but Mrs. Entwhistle did. She said it was very helpful."

"I'm using the blank sides of the pages to take notes on," said Betsy.

"Oh." Eve looked at the notebook with a different, more respectful air. "Okay. What do you want to ask me?"

"I want you to tell me about yesterday. Where were you when Belle died?"

Eve swallowed hard. "I was on my way up to see her."

"Why did you want to see her?"

"I was going to kill her."

Twenty-One

✿❀✿❀✿

Sunday, December 16, 9:07 A.M.

❄ "And did you?" asked Jill, when Betsy found she could
not speak.

"No." Eve frowned and rubbed her knuckles in the
auburn curls over her left ear as if to stimulate her brain to
make more words. "It's hard to explain, now. You see, I went
crazy while I was working for Belle and Cherry. It wasn't
Cherry's fault, not at all. I mean, she was kind of moody, so
I thought she was going to be the difficult one, but at her
worst, she was still pretty much fair. Belle—she was slicker
than snot on a doorknob, excuse my French. She started out
nice, and then became more than a boss, almost more than a

friend. She helped me to get my act together, got me to take night classes and get my GED, and go on a diet. Showed me the kind of clothes I should wear. Even my hair, the color it is now, that was her idea. It was like I turned into a whole different person—a smart person who looked pretty. And all the while, she was laying for me."

"How do you know this?" asked Betsy.

"Because of what happened. Belle encouraged me to try to get an associate degree, so I started night school." She paused to frown, thinking. "I'm only a dozen credits short, I should go finish that, shouldn't I? Anyway, at night school I met Jack. I brought him to a party she was throwing, and she just went wild over him, said he was wonderful and I should make some big moves and play up to him. So I did, and to my amazement, he liked it. He liked *me*. We started dating and we fell in love. We had a sweet little wedding— Belle was my maid of honor—and three months later I found out I was going to have his baby. It was like a dream, or a really good movie. But Belle liked Jack, too, and she started playing up to him, and then she fell in love with him, and that made her hate me, and she worked on him and against me until she got him away from me. I couldn't fight her, she knew me—she *made* me, so she knew all my weak spots. I lost Jack, and I was so angry and scared I lost the baby . . ."

Eve's beautiful eyes filled with tears.

"We're so sorry," said Betsy.

"No, no, it's all right. This is good, I can cry about it now. I couldn't before."

"Couldn't cry?"

"Not one tear. I told you—I went crazy. Insane. Out of my mind. Bonkers. Let me explain: I came to Belle's Samplers and More with nothing, with less than nothing. Well, I had Norah, but she was a mess, too. Allergic to everything, always sick. Then with Belle's help I got everything. *Everything*, things I never dreamed I could have. And one unexpected result: When I got my act together, Norah stopped being sick all the time. I never realized that my being a mess was most of the reason she was a mess. Then Belle, who had given it all to me, took it all away. My job, my pride, Jack, the baby growing under my heart. My mind couldn't take it in. I cracked. I couldn't put myself back together in Milwaukee, so I packed up Norah and went to stay with my mother in Savannah.

"My mother took me and Norah in, but after a month of my sitting on the couch eating, she told me I had to get a job. The only thing I was any good at was stitching, so I got a job at the Silver Thimble. That helped, I could act sane even if I wasn't sane. Then Mrs. Entwhistle said she wanted one of us to come to Nashville Market with her, and I just *knew* I had to come. I said I'd pay half my ticket and half my room if she'd pick me. Because I *knew* Belle would be here. And if I saw her, I was going to kill her. I knew that, too."

"Yet you came anyway," said Jill.

"Oh, yes." Eve's eyes glowed and her lips thinned. "I wasn't going to miss a chance like this. I had it all worked out. I left her a note as soon as we got here, and—"

"Left who a note?" interrupted Jill.

"Belle," Eve said, impatient with her. "I asked was she here, and the lady on the desk said yes, and I said could I leave her a note, and she said yes, so I left a note that said I wanted to talk to her and could she come to my room at ten o'clock on Saturday." Eve smiled faintly. "I just knew she'd come, I had it all worked out." She shrugged and frowned. "Except she didn't come. I couldn't believe it, I was in here at ten till, and at quarter past she still wasn't here. I thought, 'Maybe she thought I meant her suite, not mine,' so I decided to go up to her place on nine. So up I go—"

"Did you take the elevator or the stairs?" asked Jill.

Eve said impatiently, "The elevator."

"Which side?"

Eve frowned at this exasperating nit-picking. "When you come out of this suite, go right. 'Cause this suite is a little closer to the right side. Anyway, I went up on the elevator and it stops and the door opens and there's this horrible scream going on down, and a big smash at the bottom. Horrible." Eve swallowed and touched her mouth with the back of one hand. "Horrible," she repeated, taking the hand away. And again, "Horrible." She drew a deep breath and let it out in a sudden huff.

"I had what I wanted, which was Belle dead on the floor. But I didn't do it. So it was like perfect, you know? She was dead but I wasn't guilty of murder." Tears began to flow from her eyes. "And see? I can cry, isn't that great? I can cry real tears. I couldn't cry one tear for almost a whole year, but I can cry now anytime I want."

Betsy looked down at her notebook and wrote, *Insane?* She looked up again and said, "If you didn't throw her over that railing, who did?"

Eve, sniffing, raised eyebrows at her, surprised. "No one. She jumped." She wiped tears away with her fingertips. "Everyone knows that she jumped."

"Any idea why?"

"No." Eve shook her head, then offered a sly smile. "Maybe because I was coming up to see her, and she was scared?" The look in her eye made Betsy very uncomfortable.

But Jill asked quietly, in her common-sense voice, "Do you really think that might be the case?"

Eve looked a bit ashamed of herself. "No, not really. I don't know what happened. It was unreal, I can't help talking about it like it's a story someone made up. My whole life since I met Belle has been like a story, like magic or sorcery or something. She bewitched me, she was like a devil disguised as an angel, and I was going up there to kill her, and she fell dead without my having to commit murder. It was like, for once, I had the magic warrior on my side."

"Did you go to the end of the gallery? Maybe just to look?"

"No. Well, yes. I went to the other end, not the end she fell from."

"Did you see anyone up there?"

"No. Well, I thought I did, but when I looked harder, there wasn't anything. Maybe it was her wicked soul fleeing her body after she jumped."

"You aren't serious," Jill said.

Eve looked abashed. "No."

Jill persisted, "Seriously, what did you see?"

"I don't know, just a kind of rolling movement, something dark. For just a second." She shrugged. "It was my imagination, I guess, because it was just so brief and then it wasn't there. So I went down the stairs. I didn't want anyone to see me."

Betsy thought briefly and asked, "Because you thought someone might be there? Someone who might think you murdered Belle?"

Eve hesitated. "Yes."

"Do you know Lenore King?"

"You mean the designer? Yes, I remember her from

Milwaukee. Belle was always telling her she should try to sell her designs. Good to see she finally did."

"You didn't see her up on nine, did you?"

Eve squinched her eyes at Betsy. "No, why?"

"No reason."

Jill asked, "Did you think Belle had been murdered?"

Eve looked briefly from Jill to Betsy. "No, I thought—I *knew*—she had jumped. I just didn't want to be blamed for it."

Betsy asked, "Why are you so sure she jumped?"

"Well, it is funny that she did, because Belle never struck me as the suicidal type. And I don't think anyone who knew her would believe she jumped. But you see, there wasn't any-one up there with her, so she must've jumped. Was Lenore mad at her, too?"

Jill said, "We haven't talked to her yet. What about that dark shape you saw?"

"Oh, that couldn't've been a person, it was too short and too"—she gestured with her hands "—you know. People are tall and narrow, this was, er, boxy." Her hands moved again, defining a square shape.

"But you didn't go for a look," said Jill.

"No. I decided I would go quietly down the stairs and back to my room. I went down two flights, I was sure I went down twice, and when I came out, I felt faint and had to sit down on the floor. And then I started to cry. It was wonder-ful, crying like that, like I was watering my dried-up soul. Then you"—she lifted her chin at Betsy—"came along and told me I was on the eighth floor, not the seventh. It was weird, but everything was weird right then. Weirder than usual, and weird *was* usual for me, for a long time. You were so nice to me, and you walked me down to my room and told me to lie down for awhile. So I did, and Mrs. Entwhistle came in at noon and found me, and was she ever mad, because I was supposed to be shopping, and I only went into four places before I went up to wait for Belle."

"Is Mrs. Entwhistle still angry with you?"

"No. I explained, a little, about how I used to work for Belle and was waiting for her to come down and see me when this happened. That's one of those lies of omission, you see." She smiled slyly. "The kind where you leave out certain parts."

Betsy was feeling uncomfortable with this still-weird person. But she continued with her questions. She asked, "Apart from this boxy shape you saw moving down the gallery, did you see anything else unusual?"

Eve thought briefly. "Does a door closing count?"

"You saw a door close?" asked Betsy.

"I . . . think so." She raised her eyes to the ceiling, frowning.

"Which door?"

"I'm not sure. A door to a suite not far from the middle, but not in the middle. I think. It wasn't on the end."

"Are you sure you saw the door move?"

"I'm not sure about anything, no. I just kind of think I saw something that may have been a door closing the last two inches just as I looked. It could have been the way the light was coming through the skylights. The snow was making the light kind of twinkle, wasn't it?" She shrugged.

"You didn't see someone going into that room and closing the door," prompted Jill.

"No, no, nothing like that. I didn't see anyone at all. What I think it was, was someone heard the scream and peeped out, but when no one was there, they just closed their door again."

"Would that person have been in time to see the 'rolling thing'?" Betsy asked.

Eve blinked at her. "Well, yes, I suppose so. But they would have to be crazy like me, wouldn't they?"

❄ As Jill and Betsy went back up to their suite, Jill said, "Okay, Miss Sleuth, tell me what you think of Eve."

"She made me uncomfortable. It's dangerous to feel you're living in a dream or a novel, because the rules and restraints of real life don't apply. A person who felt nothing was real would be capable of anything."

Jill, after a silence of several seconds, said, "That's as damning a statement as I've heard from you about this."

Betsy drew her shoulder up a trifle. "I know. And while she was talking about me helping her yesterday, I suddenly remembered what she was wearing."

"What was that?"

"Dark slacks and sweater. The sweater had silver metallic threads woven into it. I noticed when I helped her to her feet how the bright silver twinkled against the dark wool."

"Oh, that *is* bad. Puts her at the top of the list, doesn't it? Do you think she's insane?"

"I think she believes she is."

Jill fell silent again for a bit. Then, "She says Belle took her husband from her because she fell in love with him. Cherry says it's because Belle was jealous of Eve. That's a contradiction. Who's wrong?"

"I'm not sure either one is. They're both telling the truth about what they think motivated Belle. Either way, the result was the same: Eve lost her husband to Belle."

Jill fell silent for nearly a minute. "It's like the twilight zone, trying to get inside Eve's head. Do you suppose she crawled on all fours down the gallery after she threw Belle over and now remembers it as if she saw it from a distance?"

Betsy's eyebrows lifted. "I wonder if that's not exactly what happened. What's the term? Disassociation, when the crazy person sees someone else doing a deed they actually did themselves."

Jill sighed. "We don't seem to be making a lot of progress, do we? Cherry is lying and her emotions are all over the place; Eve thinks she's crazy, and actually may be. We now have two really good suspects."

"Maybe we'll do better with Lenore," said Betsy, pulling out the card that opened the door to their suite. Again, Jill made the phone call.

Lenore King wasn't in her suite, or at least not answering her phone. Jill and Betsy went down to Bewitching Stitches and found her there, very animated, talking to three customers at once. Her dark brown hair was in a casual knot on top of her head; tendrils drifted down her temples and in front of her ears. She wore a sky-blue, long-sleeved knit dress with winter birds, chickadees, and cardinals, stitched in silk on the sleeves and yoke.

The model was droopier than ever, but Lenore seemed able to ignore its failings while pointing out its interesting arrangement of stitches and the cleverness of its design as a Christmas tree. As they approached, Lenore looked up at them.

"Oh, hello!" she said. "I'm sorry, but I've talked to so many people today that I've forgotten your names, which is too bad, because I especially want to thank you"——she addressed this to Jill—"for telling me to get back on the job. People have been so kind, and we're selling lots of my Christmas tree sampler." She picked up a pen and scribbled her name on one of the patterns and gave it to a customer, who smiled and thanked her. "And here's a free chart, just for you," she added, handing a sheet of paper to the customer.

"I'll take two of the Christmas tree, if you'll autograph both of them," said the second, and Lenore, blushing prettily, complied. She even autographed the freebie, since it was another of her designs.

The third buyer was with the second and they went to pay for their purchases together.

"This is so much better than I'd hoped for," Lenore said, happily. But then her face tightened and she added in an angry undertone, "I'm only sorry Belle can't be here to see it."

"How sure are you that Belle deliberately failed to get your model ready on time?" asked Betsy, also speaking quietly.

Lenore looked around for eavesdroppers, and Betsy stooped to bring them more nearly face to face. Lenore murmured, "I'm positive. She knew what I was designing; she knew what I wanted to do with it; she knew Bewitching Stitches wanted to sell it here at the Market; she knew the Market was moved back two months; and besides all that I came in and left her a note! What else could it be but deliberate?" she concluded.

Jill also stooped and asked quietly, "Where were you when Belle died?"

Her tone was matter of fact, but Lenore could not have been more taken aback if Jill had struck her in the face. "What do you mean?"

"Nothing except what I'm asking: Where were you when Belle died?"

Lenore looked around again and lowered her voice even

more, so that Betsy more read her lips than heard her say, "I don't want to talk about that here."

"Fine," Jill said, rising. "Come on out of here with us. This will take maybe five minutes."

"But I can't . . ." She looked around again.

Jill turned toward the table being used as a checkout counter and said to the man sitting there, "Lenore's taking a little break with us. We won't be gone long."

He looked up from filling out an order, waved his pen at her and said, "Fine, fine."

"Come on," said Jill, in that cop voice that did not even consider disobedience. Even Betsy could not resist, she rose and followed Jill out the open door of the suite, not in the least surprised to find Lenore behind her once out in the hall.

"Where shall we go?" asked Betsy, because the crowd pressed in on all sides.

"Our suite," said Jill, and she turned toward the end of the gallery and again down toward one of the stairwells in a back corner.

Up they climbed, and up, Jill tirelessly, Lenore almost as carelessly, Betsy laboring behind. Water aerobics three mornings a week were obviously not enough if there was all this stair climbing in her future, she thought despairingly.

At last Jill opened a door and they were on eight. Betsy tried to keep her breathing as effortless as Jill's and Lenore's but couldn't, and so lagged a bit behind so they wouldn't hear her unhappy lungs trying to catch up. Still, she was almost back to normal by the time they reached the suite, which was a good thing, as the other two kindly waited for her.

In the sitting room, Jill headed for the coffeepot and said over her shoulder, "May I offer you a cup of coffee, Lenore?"

"No, thank you. Let's get this done, okay?" She went to the couch and plumped down unhappily.

Jill poured herself a cup and pulled a chair away from the round table, giving it an expert flip so it turned on one leg to face Lenore. She sat down.

Betsy hastily took the other chair at the table and opened her booklet to a blank page. At the top of the opposite page was printed: Get Them Talking and Keep Them Talking! And below that a list of open-ended questions designed to get a prospective employee to reveal him- or herself. Because there was only silence in the room, Betsy read one of them out loud: "What's the worst decision you ever made?"

Lenore snorted faintly. "What kind of question is that?"

"It's an interesting question," Jill said. "Could you answer it?"

"The worst decision I ever made? Listening to Belle Hammermill!"

"Why?" asked Betsy.

"Because she was only pretending to be my friend! She didn't give a rat's bee-hind about my designs! She was just setting me up!"

"For what?"

"For *this!* So I'd work myself half to death and then come here without the one thing I needed to—" She cut herself off with a sob, and covered her eyes with one hand, waving the other at them to ask them to wait while she pulled herself together.

"That doesn't make any sense, does it?" she asked at last. "She didn't know I would come up with a design that complicated, how could she? And yet, it seemed as if she was just waiting for me to do something really great so she could spoil it! God, I was so *angry!* I've never been that angry before, it made me sick, literally. I couldn't eat, I couldn't sleep. Thank God for Priceline's cheap airfares, I was in no shape to drive to Nashville."

"Did you see Belle after you arrived here?" asked Jill.

"No." Lenore shook her head just a little longer than necessary to underline the negative.

"Did you try to?" asked Betsy.

"Oh, God!" said Lenore, and covered her eyes again. The silence grew and grew.

"Yes." It came very quietly. "I was sitting in Bewitching Stitches, and my working model looked like it had been played with by cats under a dusty bed. I just knew it would be a failure. You don't know—" She looked up at them suddenly. "You *don't* know, do you? I'm a stay-at-home mom. I love it, I don't think there's any job on earth I'd like as much or find as rewarding. But we can't afford only one breadwinner, and with both kids in school, I'm running out of excuses. I told Cody I had this great idea, that maybe I could sell it to a company that would pay good money for it. That maybe it could be the start of a real career as a pattern designer. And he said, all right, if you can sell this pattern for a decent price, you can try your hand at designing instead of going back to standing behind a cash register all day."

"So this was really, really important," said Betsy, "and Belle knew it."

"Of course she knew it! If it wasn't important, she wouldn't have bothered to"—she held up two fingers on each hand to scratch quote marks in the air—"*forget* to change the due date."

"Did you do something to make her angry at you?"

"Obviously. Problem is, I have no idea what it was. We were friends, she was so helpful and encouraging, she was behind me all the way, then suddenly she wasn't. Suddenly she didn't think the pattern was ready to submit; suddenly she was sure Bewitching Stitches wasn't the right place to send it; suddenly I was a little idiot to think I could turn out a piece worthy of professional handling—suddenly, suddenly, suddenly! And suddenly I didn't have a model fit to bring to Nashville."

"So you decided to go have it out with her," said Jill.

"Yes, dammit, yes! I knew she was here, I saw her at breakfast. So I spilled coffee on myself in Bewitching Stitches' suite to give me an excuse to leave. I went up to my suite and changed clothes and my hairstyle, and washed my makeup off. I went to the door, yanked it open, and closed it again—with me still in the room. I opened it again, and closed it again. I think I did that about five times before I decided I didn't have the nerve to go after the woman. I was so *mad* at myself! My babies, my wonderful babies, put into the hands of base-wage, daycare strangers! And it was all that ugly witch's fault! And why? *Why?* I couldn't understand why she would do that to me! And I couldn't understand why I didn't have the courage to go and stomp her into the floor like the cockroach she was!" Lenore's hands were shaking and she began to cry.

Jill walked out of the room into the back.

"So you didn't go after her," said Betsy.

"No, I didn't. I can't tell you how disappointed I was that I didn't."

Jill came back with several sheets of tissue, which she handed to Lenore.

"Thanks," said Lenore, dabbing and then blowing. "What a wreck I am! And a cowardly wreck to boot!"

"How did you find out Belle was dead?"

"I heard this noise, like a scream or yell, then a lot of voices shouting. I was sitting on my couch at that point, crying and ashamed, so at first I didn't care. But the shouting got louder and people were sounding really scared and I kept remembering that scream, like someone falling, so I finally came out. And when I looked over the railing, I could sort of see someone down on the floor with lots of people standing around her. I'm nearsighted but I don't like to wear glasses except for driving, so I couldn't see who it was. I remember I actually said to myself, 'A shame that isn't Belle.' Because she's the kind of person nothing bad ever happens to."

"When did you find out it was actually Belle who had died?"

"When I went back down to Bewitching Stitches to get my model. Someone in there was talking about it, and said it was a shop-owner from Milwaukee who had died. I turned around and went right back out again, back up to my room, and I stayed there until lunchtime. I want to thank you, Jill, for getting me back to work. They were wondering where I was, a lot of people had questions about the pattern." She sniffed and blew one last time, and then suddenly she smiled through her tears. "You know, I almost think that horrible model has turned into a selling point. People just have to stop and look to see if it's as bad as it looks. So when I was there to talk about how the real model didn't get finished in time and this was the working model, that gave me a chance to explain how I figured out the pieces. And people were interested! We've sold enough that Mr. Moore says he hopes my new design is as clever as this one." She nodded once, sharply. "I don't know if it's as clever as the Christmas tree, but it is clever, and it's almost ready for me to send to him."

She looked at Jill, then Betsy, her eyes shining. "I'm glad I'm a coward, isn't that strange?"

Betsy said, "All right, it wasn't you. Who else is here who was mad at Belle?"

Lenore drew a big breath and held it while she thought. "Well, Cherry is, I think. I mean, she's never said anything, but sometimes I'd come in and the atmosphere was pretty frosty. You could just tell they'd had words."

"What about?" asked Jill.

Lenore shrugged. "Cherry never said. Belle kind of hinted that Cherry wasn't pulling her weight, but she never said anything specific to me. But I think the strain was getting worse between the two of them."

"Very good," said Jill with a nod. "All right, who else?"

Lenore thought. "Someone who's here? I can't think of anyone."

"Did you ever hear of an employee named Eve Suttle?" asked Betsy.

"There used to be someone who worked for Belle and Cherry named Eve, I remember her because she really got her act together while she was working for them. There was some kind of kerfuffle with her after she got married, but I don't know any details. And she left a long time ago, she doesn't work for them anymore."

Twenty-Two

Sunday, 10:00 A.M.

They think it's murder, and I don't think they're convinced I didn't do it. I have to find a way to stop them. No, not that, I won't do that again. That was unbelievably worse than I thought it would be. My stomach hurts all the time and that scream keeps going on and on in my head. It won't stop. On the other hand, I'm not sorry she's gone, there is relief happening, too. Maybe the relief will get stronger and the sickness will go away.

But what am I going to do about those two women? Their questions are like enemy soldiers in computer games, you shoot one down and another takes its place. They're going to figure it out if we don't

*get out of here—and we can't get out of here because of the snow. I
wish I could just tell them I won't talk to them anymore. But I
can't do that, it would make them sure I did it.*

*Maybe if all of us stopped answering her questions . . . I'm go-
ing to talk to them.*

Sunday, 10:40 A.M.

"What have we got?" asked Jill. They were back in their
suite.

"Nothing," said Betsy in a hollow voice.

It was partly that Betsy was tired, but it was mostly
that when Betsy had another question she wanted to ask
Eve, they'd gone searching for her on three and, naturally, found her at the far end of the gallery. She'd stared at
them with wide, frightened eyes and said, "I've decided
I'm not going to talk to you anymore. Okay? So please just
go away."

"Whose idea was this?" asked Jill, but Eve just turned
and walked off.

So they were back in their suite, and Betsy was depressed.

Jill said, "You've got a notebook full of notes. That's not
nothing. Look at them, what do they tell us?"

Betsy opened the booklet, and found herself looking at a
page of notes from the interview with Cherry Pye. She read
a note at random, gave a quiet little gasp, and read the
words aloud. " 'Thought it was a prank.' "

"Who did?"

"Cherry. When she heard Belle's scream. And the smash
on the floor."

"Well, so what?"

"That was another of Cherry's lies."

"That's a lie?" said Jill, surprised. "She said she thought it was a prank and she didn't want to go gaping like a tourist. What's wrong with that?"

"Did you think it was a prank?"

"Me? No, of course not." Jill shook her head, remembering. "I was out of the suite before I thought anything, looking over the railing. But I'm a cop, Betsy; that's different."

"I'm not a cop, and the racket I heard all around me after she fell was not people being amused or startled, they were scared, and then horrified," said Betsy. "But Cherry said she didn't look down until she was in the elevator and heard two women say someone had died in a fall."

"Maybe she's a—I don't know—a social inept, or something. Someone who doesn't interpret people's behavior accurately."

"You think she's autistic?" Betsy was incredulous.

Jill frowned and lifted her shoulders. "Well, no. And you're right, she'd almost have to be, to ignore all the shouts and screams. Wouldn't she?"

"So why did she say that? Did she have some other reason for not going to look?"

"Maybe she couldn't see over the railing and for some reason doesn't want to say that. You know, it would be just one more admission of something she can't do that fully abled people can do without thinking."

"Maybe. But that's a pretty thin argument," said Betsy, and a thoughtful silence fell.

"On the other hand, look at her chair," said Betsy, at last. "Those plastic spokes don't twinkle like wire wheels do."

"You think that twinkle business Judy Bialic told you

about is for real? I thought when Eve described the way the falling snow made the light twinkle . . ."

"Yes, but she also said she saw some kind of movement. Someone was up there, we know that; someone who threw Belle over the railing. It's true, I didn't see anyone standing up there, and nobody else did, either. I know, I know, you can't see someone who isn't right up against the railing. But it's funny." Betsy thought a few seconds. "Eve said the shape was boxy, not long. I wonder . . ." she hesitated. "What do you call it when you do this?" Betsy held the back of her skirt in place with her hands, then stooped and awkwardly waddled a few steps, her knees nearly up to her chin.

Jill put a hand over her mouth to hide a grin. "Duck walk," she said, and held out her other hand to help Betsy up.

Betsy grabbed and pulled herself upright. "My joints don't want me to do things like that anymore," she sighed, shaking a leg to loosen an incipient cramp. "But Eve is a young woman, she could duck walk all the way to the stairwell if she had to. Farther, probably. And she was wearing a dark sweater with lots of silver threads knit into it."

"But Eve's the one who said the shape was boxy."

"So it was Lenore she saw."

"And what would have possessed Lenore to think of doing something like that?"

Betsy thought. "Well, picture it. Belle's scream brought almost everyone's attention. If I had set off that scream, I'd've ducked down instinctively. And once down, it's easy to think maybe I should stay down."

"Yes, I can see that," agreed Jill, but doubtfully. "Still, a duck walk is . . . I don't know . . ."

"Silly?" said Betsy.

"You said it, not me," agreed Jill, suddenly fighting to contain her amusement again.

Betsy made a sulky face. "I don't like it when you laugh at me."

"I'm not laughing," said Jill, which was true—but she was smiling. "But think about it: If the twinkle is real, then it can't be Cherry, because she doesn't have wheels that twinkle. I'm just happy because we've finally crossed someone off the list, even if it does call for someone else to duck walk away from the scene of the crime."

"Well, okay," said Betsy. And she smiled, because she had looked silly doing her duck walk. "Anyway Eve was wearing slacks, no need to duck walk when you can crawl."

"Did Lenore she have anything about her that twinkled?"

"I don't remember anything, but she changed clothes before she came down to lunch, remember? She told us about that, how she changed out of her fancy working clothes because she spilled coffee on them."

"So maybe we should find out, if we can, what she was wearing that morning," said Jill.

"Let's go back to Bewitching Stitches and ask her."

They found her in her sky-blue dress oramented with birds and waited until a pair of shoppers walked away before approaching her, but she waved them off. "I'm not talking to you anymore. You're not official, and I don't have to answer your questions."

"Whose idea was this?" asked Jill, but Lenore set her jaw into a stubborn line and looked away until they left her alone.

So they went to speak to Mr. Moore, the owner. He seemed proud and possessive of Lenore.

"She's doing great for us, now she's seen how well her pattern is selling," he said. "You should have seen her yesterday morning, she was so unhappy."

"Was she dressed as beautifully as she is right now?" asked Betsy.

"Oh, gosh, yes," he replied.

"What was she wearing? Do you remember?"

He thought that an odd question, but obediently tried to recall. "She had this long green skirt, and a fancy burgundy blouse with trick sleeves, and her hair was done up with little slips of it hanging down. Very classy, but even more so today. Look at her over there, she dresses like a queen."

"Was there gold or silver in the blouse or skirt?" persisted Betsy.

He frowned at her. "No. Everything was plain, not even shiny. What's this about?"

"We're looking for someone who was wearing clothing that twinkled yesterday."

"Well, it wasn't her."

"Thank you, sir," said Jill, and the two left the suite.

"Well?" said Betsy.

Jill said, "Looks like we really are down to one, then. Unless you want to search Lenore's room? But I can't imagine someone putting on flashy clothing to go commit a murder."

"I think you're right."

"So, it wasn't Cherry, and it wasn't Lenore. That leaves Eve Suttle. I guess now we go call Sergeant Birdsong and tell him what we've got."

"Yeah."

"You don't sound happy about it."

"I know. And I should be, shouldn't I? But there's still

something . . ." She gnawed her bottom lip briefly. "Let's go talk to Mr. Kreinik and Mr. Stott."

The Kreinik suite was a riot of color in displays of floss in silk, cotton, wool, and blends, and glittering metallics of every thickness and color, on cards or as skeins. Doug, in an open-collared shirt, was standing in the middle of the room talking to another man, gesturing with hands and forearms so as not to knock anything over. He saw them come in and smiled over the top of the man's head. "I'll be right with you," he said.

And he was. "How can I help you?" he asked.

"About yesterday," began Betsy.

He took a step back, looking Jill up and down, then Betsy. "Oh, are you the two going around looking into that unfortunate death?"

"Yes, sir," said Jill.

Betsy said, "We just want to know—"

"I don't think I should talk to anyone who's not a police official," interrupted Doug.

"I'm a police official," said Jill, producing her ID and badge. "Sergeant Jill Larson." She snapped the wallet shut before he could get a good look at it.

He studied her closely, but Jill could absorb any amount of study without flinching, and at last he nodded. "All right, ask your questions."

Jill stepped back to let Betsy come forward. "Yesterday, you were warning people about Belle Hammermill's unethical behavior," she began.

"Illegal behavior," he corrected her.

"You're right, illegal behavior," she agreed. "But you were also telling that story about the woman who didn't know who you were and told you to your face what she thought was a funny story about how difficult Kreinik blending filament is to use."

Doug smiled. "That was later, after Ms. Hammermill's fall."

"You're sure you didn't tell it earlier, perhaps shortly before she died?"

He ran a big hand across his curly dark hair. "No, I'm sure I didn't. Why, is that important?"

"I think it may be. Now, when you ran out of the suite to look at what happened, to see Belle on the floor, did you look around?"

"Do you mean, did I look up, like to see where she fell from? I don't think so, but I don't remember if I did or not."

"No, I mean did you look around the gallery here on six? What I'm after is someone who saw a woman in a wheelchair near your suite."

He frowned at her. "A woman in a wheelchair," he repeated. "No—wait, do you mean Emily Watson? She came by this morning."

"You know Emily Watson?"

"Certainly. She's co-chair of the INRG committee that runs the Market."

"No, this is a different person. She didn't come into your suite, but she was near it, moving down the gallery toward the elevators."

He thought briefly, then shook his head. "I'm sorry, I don't remember seeing her. But I couldn't tell you if there was any specific person nearby or not. Well, except Dave Stott. He and I were talking in here when it happened, and he came out with me to look over the railing. He seemed to be looking around. You might talk to him."

"Thank you, we will," said Betsy.

"Thank you, sir," added Jill.

They left the suite and Betsy said, "No help there. Are we expecting too much? It was chaotic when it happened, all the shouting and screaming."

Jill replied, "Yes, but when something awful happens, people go into alarm mode, and they notice things, you'd be surprised what they notice. A person in a wheelchair isn't common, and it isn't wrong to think someone may have seen her."

Dave Stott's suite did not face the atrium, but was down one of the short passages leading to a stairwell. Norden Crafts had a two-bedroom suite, and was using both the sitting room and one of the bedrooms to display its wares. There was a wide variety of charts, fabrics, and specialty items. Not just scissors and needles, but pillow forms, and books, and small wooden and metal boxes with inset tops of evenweave fabric. Dave was sitting on a couch explaining the use of an esoteric gadget to a customer while his wife filled out a sales form at a table across the room. There were a lot of customers crowding the rooms, but at last they emptied, and Betsy sat down next to Dave. He smiled at her. "Can I help you?" he asked.

"I want to ask you some questions about yesterday, when you were over in the Kreinik suite."

"What about it?" He turned his head to look up at Jill. "Are you two together?"

"Yes, sir, I'm Sergeant Jill Larson, and we're conducting an informal investigation into Belle Hammermill's death."

"I thought it was an accident."

"We're trying to find out just exactly how it happened," said Betsy.

"All right. What do you want to ask me?"

"Do you know you look a whole lot like General Ulysses S. Grant?" asked Betsy.

He laughed out loud. "I've been told that before. My wife and I have a vacation home near Galena, Illinois, which was General Grant's hometown. But what has that got to do with Belle Hammermill?"

"Nothing," said Betsy, blushing. "I just suddenly realized the resemblence. Sorry. What I really wanted to ask you was: "What were you and Dave talking about when it happened?""

Dave said slowly, "About how Belle Hammermill cheated him."

"I thought so. Now, did you look up to the place where Belle fell?"

He nodded once, sharply. "As a matter of fact, I did. I guess I was thinking the railing broke. But I didn't see a broken railing."

"Did you see anyone up there?"

"Well, it depends on where she fell from."

"The top floor. Nine," said Betsy.

He nodded. "Okay, that's what we thought. And no, there wasn't anyone up there, not right over where she landed. There were people looking over the railings all around the atrium, but none along the side she must've fallen from, if she fell from nine."

"Did you see anything up there at all?" asked Jill.

He looked around and up at her. "No, I don't think so."

"Nothing moving along the railing?"

He thought briefly. "No," he said, but doubtfully. "What do you mean moving along the railing? You mean like someone running?"

"We have a report of someone or something moving along the gallery up there. Something that twinkled or flashed."

He shook his head. "I don't remember anything like that. But I didn't stare up at the place; I looked up, then down again."

Betsy asked, "Did you see a woman in a wheelchair outside the Kreinik suite when you went out to see what was going on?"

"No, I wasn't paying close attention—well, wait a minute, I did look up and down the gallery." He thought a bit. "Everyone was at the railing, shouting and pointing. I don't remember anyone in a wheelchair, and I think I should have noticed it. But maybe not, people were coming out of the suites and the galleries were getting clogged. I could have missed it, if she was down aways, hidden by all the people coming out of the suites. I wasn't looking too closely, anyway. I was shook up by all this. It was about the worst thing I've ever seen in my life, that woman down on the floor." He pinched his eyes closed with thumb and forefinger, lifting his eyeglasses to get at them. "It was really awful."

"Yes, sir, I'm sure it was a bad thing to see," said Jill.

Betsy stood. "Thank you, Mr. Stott." She put out her hand.

He took it and his eyes ran over her name tag. "Hey, I know you! You took over that needlework shop in Excelsior from Margot Berglund. I heard she died suddenly. That's too bad; she was a good businesswoman."

"Yes, she was. She was my sister."

"Is that right? Well, you seem to be doing all right up there. Continued success to you."

"Thank you."

He appeared ready to say something else, but Jill hustled Betsy away, out the door of the suite.

"I bet he's wondering how you manage to be a cop and run a needlework shop at the same time," said Jill.

"I don't think we should go back and explain, do you?"

"No. Where are we going now?"

"I want to talk to Emily Watson."

"What about?"

"Wheelchairs."

Emily was in her usual place behind the long table INRG members had checked in at when they arrived. At this late stage no one was checking in, so she and another committee member were stitching and talking. There was a scatter of paper on the table, extra Market Guides, room service menus, a Nashville phone book, a couple of free counted cross-stitch patterns. Another table set at a right angle to Emily's had stacks of T-shirts and canvas carrier bags for sale.

Emily was working on a small Celtic knot pattern in gold, wine, and green, with black backstitching. Betsy recognized the chart as one from Textile Heritage, a Scottish company.

There was a chair on Betsy and Jill's side of the table, at a gesture from Jill, Betsy took it. She opened her Hiring and Management notebook.

"That was a good class," noted Emily.

"Yes, I'm finding all sorts of useful things in the booklet; I wish I'd been here for the class. Emily, may we ask you some questions?"

"Certainly." Emily tucked her needle into the white

222   *Monica Ferris*

evenweave fabric of her piece and prepared to pay close attention.

"You said earlier that the lightweight, armless wheelchair isn't suitable for shopping."

"Yes, that's right," nodded Emily. "You don't have anyplace to put your purchases except on your lap, and without arms on the chair to stop them, they tend to slide off onto the floor. They're good in the shop, though, because they're lightweight, which makes them easy to propel hour after hour. And they turn on a dime, and they're just a little narrower than the heavier chairs, so you're not constantly nicking the furniture."

"How likely is it that someone might come to the Market with two chairs, a lightweight one and a heavier one?"

Emily's eyebrows rose. "I suppose it's possible, but not likely. Well, if I was going out more than once, you know, to a museum or something, I might bring both."

"If you had to bring just one, is there any reason it would be just the lighter one?"

"No," replied Emily at once. "If I brought just one—and I did—I'd bring the one I could go shopping in. Now if I were a vendor, that would be different, of course. But any shop-owner in a wheelchair would bring the bigger chair, probably one with a basket."

"Well, thank you, that's what we wanted to know."

"You're welcome," said Emily, puzzled. "I hope I helped."

"Yes, you did." Betsy stood. "Thanks again."

Emily looked at Jill inquiringly. Jill just shrugged her own puzzlement and followed Betsy away.

But when they got in the elevator, Jill said, "You think she has a second chair in her suite?"

"If she does . . ."

"Let's go ask her."

But Cherry had joined the conspiracy of silence and she refused to even answer the question, much less let them into her suite to see if there was a second chair.

"Like what?" asked Jill.

"Since we're up here, let's go look at the scene of the crime."

"Does it matter?" said Jill.

"I want something more than her overhearing the wrong story Doug told," said Betsy. "Something physical I can put my finger on."

Twenty-Three

Sunday, 11:35 A.M.

Betsy said, "First, let's see where Lenore and Cherry's rooms are in relation to where Belle went over."

Lenore's room was along one of the long sides, about three doors up from the twin elevators. "So it wasn't her door Eve saw closing," remarked Betsy.

"I thought Lenore was off the list."

"After Cherry got back on, I thought maybe Lenore should be there, too."

"Maybe Eve was lying about the door," said Jill. "Some people, if you press them to remember something, make something up."

"Well, maybe she wasn't. Cherry's room is just a few doors down from where Belle went over."

"Eve's only got one oar in the water, you know," said Jill.

Betsy smiled. "No, I think it's more that her boat's sprung a leak. Come on." They walked back down the gallery to the lobby end, and turned to walk along the railing toward the middle.

"She was right about here, close to the center," said Betsy, stopping. She laid a hand on the railing, gingerly. "Makes my toes ache," she murmured. "Fingers, too." She tried looking over without leaning forward, chin up and eyebrows lifted. "Long line for lunch," she noted, being able to easily see only the other end of the atrium floor. She let her eyes wander up the tiers of galleries, noting the colorful banners hanging over the railings on the lower floors. DMC read one. DRAGON FIRE DESIGNS read another. And there was KREINIK.

Jill came to lean over and look straight down, which made Betsy uncomfortable enough to back away. She kept backing until she went right into a recessed doorway, thumping it loud enough to cause her to step forward hastily, then turn to see if someone inside heard her and thought she was knocking. But no one came to the door.

"That's Belle's suite," said Jill.

"Oh? Oh, well, of course. She came out and went right to the railing to take a look."

"Could someone just walk right up to her without her noticing?"

"Let me try," said Betsy quickly, because she didn't want to be the one standing at the railing. "Go back where you were."

Jill obediently went back to lean on the railing with

widespread hands and Betsy tried coming from different directions without drawing Jill's attention.

"Well, you can't come down the long side without me seeing you," Jill concluded. "So whoever snuck up on her either came up the stairs or out of one of these doors."

"Only Cherry's room is along here," said Betsy. "Lenore's is along that long side."

"So if Lenore or Eve did it, she lay in wait, you think?"

"Yes, probably. They all knew which room she was in, didn't they?"

"Eve did, she asked at the desk. And I'll wager Cherry did, because Belle initially reserved the room for both of them."

"What a cruel thing to do!" Betsy snapped. "Cherry couldn't use the bathroom unless it was specially equipped, and Belle knew that, and knew there were special rooms for her—this was their third Market. Belle was a wicked person, there's no other word for her. The way she treated all three of them! I'm almost inclined to say good riddance to bad rubbish and just let it go on record as a freak accident."

"Do you want to do that?"

Betsy thrust her fingers into her hair. "No, I guess not," she grumbled. "I want to know for sure." She looked around. "I want to know who *didn't* do it, who the innocent ones are. Trouble is, I don't know how to figure that out."

She began walking up the gallery, just looking. Her boyfriend, a retired detective, once told her that the first thing a detective does at a crime scene is just look. Look at everything.

With no idea what she might be looking for—and the crime scene more than twenty-four hours old—Betsy had no real hope of finding anything. But she had nowhere else to go, no better ideas, so she just walked along very slowly, letting her eyes take in whatever they could find.

She paused and went for a closer look at a suite next door to Belle's. Not the door, but the frame around one of the bay windows. A little more than knee high there was a tiny gouge in the wood.

Jill, coming along behind, said, "What is it?"

Betsy looked up at the room number. "Is this one of those handicapped suites?"

"I don't know."

"Can we find out?"

"Sure." Jill got her cell phone out and went into its record of recent calls. One was to the Consulate Hotel.

A very tired voice—Marveen's—asked, "How may I help you?"

"This is Jill Cross Larson up on nine with Betsy Devonshire. Can you tell us if Room 924 is a handicap suite?"

There was a pause, possibly while Marveen drew on reserves of patience she didn't know she had. But her voice was polite as she said, "No, it isn't."

"Thank you." Jill disconnected and said to Betsy, "It isn't. Why did you want to know?"

"Because there's a nick in the wood right here, and it's right about the height where Cherry nicked the doorway on her way to the bathroom."

Jill stooped for a closer look. "Well, well, well," she said. "Nice and fresh, too. Of course, maybe Cherry—or Ms. Watson—visited someone in this room. Not Belle, this isn't her suite."

"No, someone lay in wait right here for Belle to come out." Betsy was very gently touching the little gouge that had damaged the paint and exposed raw wood. Jill straightened and hit the button to redial the front desk. "I'm so sorry to keep bothering you, but who's staying in Suite 924?" she asked, listened, and said "Thank you."

"Who?" asked Betsy.

"Kathy Knight from Galena, Illinois."

"I suppose we could ask her if she knows Cherry and had her in for a visit here at the Market."

Betsy shook her head. "Damn. I don't want it to be Cherry. I *like* her."

"I know you do. But there's also the fact that the way Belle was lifted over that railing is the *only* way Cherry could have done it. Every other way I tried, I had to be standing."

"But we need something more concrete. What we have is barely circumstantial."

"There's the gouge."

"A guest got clumsy with a suitcase," said Betsy.

"There's the conspiracy!"

"What conspiracy?"

"To stop talking to us. It had to be Cherry who did that!"

"What makes you think that?"

"It would never occur to Eve to do something like that! She *wanted* to talk to us."

"But Lenore—" started Jill.

"She didn't know Eve was here, remember?" Betsy bit her thumbnail. "It's the money, probably. Belle was stealing Cherry's money, the settlement she got for her accident. Cherry needs that money to live on." Betsy turned and walked to the railing, looking over, but not seeing anything except the details in her mind. "This whole thing is about need. Cherry needed to keep her money, Lenore needed to stay at home, Eve needed to hang onto her new self."

"And Belle?" asked Jill.

"Belle was very focused on her own needs, that's why she didn't help people because they needed help, but because it fed her ego. I'm sure she felt dependent on Cherry because of the money Cherry brought, and so stealing it was her way of declaring her independence."

"What are you, a psychiatrist?"

"I wish. Then I could help people instead of getting them arrested. Now, Jill, whose need was greatest?"

Jill grimaced. "All right, Cherry's."

Betsy nodded vigorously. "Lenore said she's already working on a new design; Eve went home to her family and got a new job. Cherry couldn't go out and get hit by another bus, could she?"

"And if she lost a big enough hunk of her settlement, she'd have to go on welfare. I can see where that prospect might make her desperate."

Betsy said, "So what do we do now? You don't have a gun or handcuffs, and the Nashville police can't get here. Should we go get a key to her suite and break in?"

Jill smiled. "Down, girl. There's no rush. Where's she going to go? Nobody can leave the hotel until the snow melts. She's safe right where she is. Let's go tell Lieutenant Birdsong what we've got."

They went down to the lobby to talk with Marveen. Marveen insisted that she be the one Sergeant Birdsong. They all retired to the chilly hotel office while Marveen placed the call to police headquarters. She was transferred around for awhile, to her increasing impatience—which she displayed only in a tendency to speak a little slower while a muscle in her jaw started to throb.

At last she hung up and said, "They'll have him call us."

Five minutes later the phone rang. Marveen snatched it

up, but "Consulate Hotel," she said in her usual business-friendly voice. Then she smiled. "Sergeant Birdsong, this is Marveen Harrison. I want to tell you that the Minnesota policewoman you said could investigate the death of Belle Hammermill says she knows who murdered her." Pause. "Mmm-hmmm, yes, murder. And she's right here."

Marveen handed the receiver to Jill. "Sergeant Larson here, sir," said Jill crisply, and listened. "Yes, we're sure, though the evidence is largely circumstantial." Pause. "We interviewed her yesterday afternoon, but she denied any involvement." Longer pause. "Well, we've since gotten more information, including an alibi that's fallen apart, and a mark left on the wall up near where Belle Hammermill was thrown over that closely resembles the marks left by the axle of a wheelchair." Pause. "Yes, sir, we're pretty confident." Longer pause. "All right, yes sir. We'll be here."

Jill hung up and said, "He wants us to wait until he can get here. He says at least an hour, maybe two. Let's go have lunch."

Godwin saw them coming and waved them to his table, where he was sitting with Terrence Nolan. Lunch was chicken soup made with split peas and noodles, or beef stew made with potatoes, carrots, and corn. And more biscuits. Beverages choices were iced tea, sweet iced tea— "You know you're in the south now," remarked Godwin—coffee, bottled water and a choice of lesser-known brands of soft drinks. Even though Jill and Betsy were among the last to arrive, there was plenty to eat.

Betsy chose the beef stew. "I wonder what we'll have for dinner?" she asked, but no one answered. The soups were good and filling, and there was an apple cobbler for dessert, à la mode, if you liked.

Godwin announced that he'd been in every suite, and bought only items sure to sell. In return, Betsy and Jill hinted to Godwin that there had been a break. He was so torn between continuing his happy flirtation with Terrence and hearing the details, that at last Terrence realized something was up, and excused himself.

Godwin watched him go with a sigh, then turned eagerly to Betsy and said, "All right, boss, dish!"

So Betsy did.

After lunch, they told Marveen they'd be waiting in their suite and went up in the elevator.

Jill had dared to annoy Marveen one more time by asking to borrow the bottle of white glue. She sat down with superb patience to finish her Santa pin, stitching the fastener on the back of a piece of maroon velvet, then gluing the velvet over the white felt. She got out her new scissors and began to trim the velvet, being careful not to cut a thread in the process.

Godwin went into his suitcase to find his knitting and worked on another of his endless series of white socks.

Betsy opened the crewel kit of grazing sheep and exclaimed over the beauty and varied textures of the fibers, then settled down to stitch a sheep with white wool, varying the direction of the long and short stitches a bit to suggest the roundness of a belly or the fullness of a chest. All the fabric offered was a thin black outline of the picture and an occasional hint about the length of the grass the sheep stood in.

They couldn't talk, there was nothing to say. At last Godwin turned on the television and found *A Christmas Story* playing on one channel. Ralphie was imagining himself saving his family from robbers by the use of his trusty Daisy air rifle.

"What do you want for Christmas, Betsy?" he asked.

"For this to be over."

The phone rang at last. Jill picked it up, listened briefly and said, "Thanks." She hung up. "Lieutenant Birdsong is in the lobby."

Godwin, to his disgust and chagrin, had to stay behind. "Ratza fratza margle shuga," he said, imitating Ralphie's father, and sat down again with his knitting to watch more of the movie, his manner rather pointed.

Birdsong was resplendent in high, lace-up rubber boots, heavy wool trousers, and red plaid hunting coat with traces of thread on the back where his hunting license had been cut off. He had hat hair. "It's warm, at least," he explained. "And my feet are dry." With him was a female police officer, creaking with authority, gunbelt, and bulletproof vest. Birdsong did not introduce her.

"Now, where is this suspect of yours?" he asked.

"We don't know," said Betsy.

He looked at her, his shaggy eyebrows raised very high. "You mean she got away?" he asked in a soft, dangerous voice.

"No, sir," said Jill. "She's in the hotel. Probably in her suite. We went up awhile ago to ask her if she had a second wheelchair with her, and while she refused to answer us, it's likely she's stayed in her suite to guard against us coming in for a look."

Jill placed a call from the house phone. "Hi, Cherry, it's Jill Cross Larson again. Still won't talk to us? All right, we understand. Yes, ma'm, thank you." Jill's voice was crisp, but polite.

Jill hung up and said, "None of our three suspects will talk to us."

They took the elevator up to nine. They had no more

than gotten off when the door to Cherry's suite opened and she rolled out. She froze on seeing Birdsong and the female police officer, started to back in, then instead rolled out and started down toward the other long side.

Jill immediately turned and ran the other way.

"Halt!" Birdsong barked. "Stop, stay where you are!" He gestured at the female police officer, who bolted out in front of him, running past the elevators.

Betsy stayed with Birdsong.

Cherry kept going, leaning so far forward she all but disappeared below the level of the railing. The wire wheels of her chair twinkled between the balusters. She reached the end of the gallery and started down the other long side. She was moving very fast, she would be at the elevators before either the uniform or Jill could reach her.

Then the chair stopped—apparently Cherry saw Jill coming up the gallery from the other end. The chair turned, only to face the uniformed woman coming toward her. She guided her chair to the railing, and her hands moved, setting the brakes.

She looked across the open space and saw Birdsong and Betsy and grinned at them. She reached up and grabbed the railing, pulling herself up.

Jill put on a burst of speed, but she was going to be too late, Betsy could see that.

Suddenly a mighty voice roared from below:

"DON'T YOU DARE!"

Cherry, disconcerted, hesitated, looked down.

So did Betsy. So did Birdsong. It was Marveen, standing

in the middle of the atrium floor, at the very end of her patience with these people.

Before she could recover, Cherry was gripped from behind by Jill. The female police officer was there two seconds later, grabbing at Cherry's fists before they could do any damage.

It was a little over an hour later before Betsy and Jill came back into the suite. Godwin was agog for details. "Tell me *everything!*" he demanded.

So Betsy began to describe dramatic arrest. "Oh, I saw that, I came to watch," said Godwin, "and I saw them take Cherry down in the elevator. Marveen should be an opera singer—what a voice!"

"I think she would have apologized if Sergeant Birdsong hadn't said she deserved a medal for it," said Betsy. "She has a strong sense of decorum and the yell was her attempt to bring it back to her hotel." Betsy smiled. "She wanted people to stop flinging themselves and others over her railings, and for the police to go away and take any riff-raff with them."

"Did Cherry confess?" asked Godwin.

"Sort of. She said maybe the scream that had been going on inside her head would shut up now."

"Oh, poor thing! Is Marveen mad at you and Jill for all this?"

"Probably," said Betsy. "But she's glad it's over. She wanted us to talk to people, answer their questions, but I said that I'd had enough of questions from Lieutenant Birdsong. I wanted to come up here. I imagine everyone in the hotel has questions for us, and I'm not up to that."

Jill snorted. "You mean people have all kinds of answers and theories. Most of them wrong."

Betsy sighed. "You know something? I don't care. I'm tired. I want to lie down in that bedroom with the lights turned off and not think about anything for awhile."

"Go ahead," said Jill. "I'm going to make a pot of coffee. We'll wake you in time for supper."

Twenty-Four
Epilogue

December 24, 8:30 P.M.

It was a white Christmas in Excelsior that year, but then, it generally is. Betsy stayed open late Christmas Eve. Tomorrow Crewel World was closed, but it was a working day. All the Christmas lights must come down, the Christmas patterns, kits and charts put away, except for a few in a special corner, up year round, and the Valentine stuff brought out. Betsy was getting used to working in advance of any holiday or season, but she didn't much like it; so it was with a little sigh that she looked around a final time at the markers of her favorite season. Too bad the custom of celebrating Christmas for twelve days wasn't followed in this modern world. And too bad that it wasn't celebrated only twelve days in advance—by the time Christmas arrived nowadays, trees and ornaments were looking decidedly tired of the whole business.

Of course, up in her apartment, the tree hadn't gone up until the previous Tuesday, so it was still fragrant and new to the eye. And it would stay up until Twelfth Night, January six.

Betsy turned on the Bose and a Christmas CD started, filling the apartment with angels heard on high singing, *"Glor, or-r-r-r-r, or-r-r-r-r, or-r-r-r-r, oria, in excelsis Deo!"* No more "It's beginning to look a lot like Christmas." Tonight was the time for the real thing. Interesting how Christmas songs were about getting ready, and Christmas carols were about the event.

Under the tree were many bright packages hinting at lavish and luxurious things. Betsy smiled at them, and went to change out of her work clothes. She came out of the bedroom wearing a peacock-green jumpsuit, a very dressy outfit that looked fine with the boots she'd need to put on before venturing out for the midnight service at Trinity.

Meanwhile, she went into the kitchen to take the filo dough in its many paper-thin layers out of the refrigerator. She cut the dough into rectangles and strewed a thin layer of steamed spinach up its center, and embellished the spinach with a few crumbles of herbed feta cheese. She rolled the rectangles up, pressed the ends shut, and put them into a pre-heated oven for twelve minutes. Shelly arrived with Mayor Jamison just as the oven timer went off. Shelly was a part-timer in Betsy's shop, an elementary school teacher the rest of the time. She was an attractive woman with masses of light brown hair done up in an elaborate way. Jamison was a

confirmed bachelor; a narrow, slender man with dark hair
and eyes, whose job as mayor was also part-time. Betsy put
Shelly to work slicing the rolled filo into thirds while she
arranged cookies on another cooking sheet. Jamison un-
corked a bottle of wine and lit the candles on the table in
the dining alcove.

Godwin arrived just as the cookies came out. His lover
went home for Christmas, a place Godwin was not allowed
to visit. He and John made up for it with a big blow-out at
New Year's.

"Kind of sad not to have Jill here," said Godwin.

"It's Lars's year," said Betsy. Lars was a Lutheran, and Jill
an Episcopalian. They alternated years of Christmas and
Easter at one another's church.

They ate the spinach hors d'oeuvres with the wine, then
tackled the cookies. Jamison wandered the apartment, looking at Betsy's tree and other ornamentation—he hadn't been
able to come to her Christmas party last week. "Say, what's
this I hear about you and Jill solving a crime down in
Nashville?" he asked in his decided midwestern twang.

"Yes," said Shelly. "You haven't told us about it."

"That's because the person I thought should have done it,
turned out to be innocent," said Betsy. "That was kind of
depressing."

Godwin said, "But you put the clues together very clev-
erly. It wouldn't have been right if the wrong person got arrested."

"Tell us about it," said Shelly. "We've got plenty of time
before we have to leave for church."

"All right." So Betsy related the events of ten days ago,
making little of her efforts. Godwin kept interupting to
correct the record, perhaps going a little far in the other

direction. It felt strange to be talking about jealousy, theft, insane hatred, wickedness, and murder on Christmas Eve, but the listeners were enrapt. When she finished, Shelly said, "Did Cherry ever explain what led her to murder Belle? I mean, I would think an audit would expose Belle's shenanigans with the cash register, so why did Cherry have to kill her?"

Betsy said, "Sergeant Birdsong took Cherry downtown to police headquarters and once there, Cherry confessed the whole thing." It was taken down as a statement, and he sent Jill a copy of it, which she let me read.

"What happened was, Cherry went to talk to Belle in her suite after breakfast. Belle was angry that Cherry was going to order an independent audit and tried to talk her out of it. But the more she argued, the more Cherry was sure Belle was stealing money from the store. And at last Belle said yes, she had been taking money—and so what? The store was half hers, she could take money out of it if she wanted to. If Cherry liked, Belle would save her the cost of the audit and give her a list of when and how much she'd taken. Cherry left in a rage. She was so angry she had to stop for a minute to regain control of herself. She heard a door open and pulled back into a doorway—the doorways were recessed deeply enough to get her mostly out of sight. She didn't want anyone to see her the way she was feeling.

"And out came Belle, all happy and smiling. She walked up to the railing and stood there like the Queen of England after the defeat of the Armada—those were Cherry's own words. And Cherry simply rolled up behind her, grabbed her by the lower legs and tossed her over. It wasn't planned or premeditated. It was a combination of rage and opportunity. She was sorry the instant it happened. But it was done, with no way to undo it. She really didn't look down at Belle on the floor until she got in the elevator, and it just made her sicker." Betsy looked at Godwin. "She said that if you'd asked her, she would have told you she did it."

"Like I was even *thinking* something like that!" exclaimed Godwin.

"She described you in her statement as a kind gentleman who was a comfort to her."

"*Brrrr* and bosh!" said Godwin, shaken to think he had given comfort to a murderer.

Jamison checked his watch. "If we want a good seat, we'd better get over there," he said.

And so out they trailed into the deep and frostbitten night, with lights glowing softly from nearly every window, lighting the way to the church, where the choir was already warming up the congregation with, "Oh, Come All Ye Faithful."

But Betsy found it hard to sing at first, lost in thoughts of the three suspects. Lenore, she considered, would be fine; she could stay at home with her children while she built a career in design. Poor Eve was more problematic. Perhaps her tears could actually water her soul back to life. But Cherry, whom she'd really thought of as sweet and down-home—Cherry's future was winter-dark indeed.

Crewel Yule Tree Ornament

Designed by Lenore Fischer of At River's End

Symbol	Anchor	Kreinik Braid	Color
•	2		White
#	85		Orchid-LT
✖	433		Ice Blue-MED
%	1038		Sky Blue
❤	9046		Christmas Red
✳		001	Kreinik # 4 Braid–Silver
a		002HL	Kreinik # 4 Braid–Gold High Lustre

FABRIC: Zweigart 28 ct. Cashel Linen—Dark Teal Green (3281-641-55)

STITCH COUNT: 58 wide × 63 high

FINISHED SIZE OF ORNAMENT: 4 1/8 w × 4 1/2 h inches
DESIGN SIZE: 28 COUNT (OVER 2): 4 1/8 w × 4 1/2 h inches
INSTRUCTIONS:

• Cut two 5 1/2 inch wide × 6 inch high pieces of linen. Find center on one piece of linen and baste using contrasting color thread along *dark dashed lines* shown on chart. This will become the sewing line when assembling the ornament.

• Stitch design as specified on the chart. Use two strands of floss or one strand of #4 Kreinik braid for cross stitches and three-quarter stitches. Use one strand of Kreinik braid for backstitches.

• Work Ray Stitches with one strand of 001 Silver Kreinik braid. Work Star Stitches with one strand of 002HL Gold High Lustre Kreinik braid. Work all other backstitching with one strand of 002HL Gold High Lustre Kreinik braid.

• Repeat the design on the other piece of fabric.

• When all stitching is completed, carefully press on wrong sides. Trim fabric 1/2 inch away from the basting line. Zigzag or stay stitch along edges to prevent fraying of the linen along the edges.

• (Optional) Cut two pieces of lightweight interfacing to match the trimmed ornament's size and shape within the basted lines. Place one piece of interfacing on *wrong* side of each ornament piece. Fuse to linen according to manufacturer's directions.

• With *right* sides of the stitched ornament facing, stitch the pieces of linen fabric together along basted line allowing 1/2 inch seams and using sewing thread to match the fabric.

Leave an opening on the bottom for turning and stuffing. Carefully clip and trim corners to reduce bulk. Turn right sides out and press. Press in 1/2 inch seam allowances on opening. Stuff lightly with polyester fiberfill. Fold in seam allowances on bottom opening and blind stitch closed with matching sewing thread.

• Attach cording or braid to top of ornament for hanger.

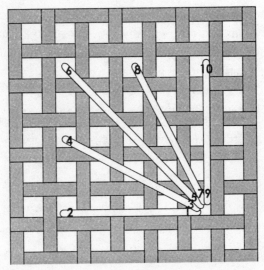

Ray Stitch

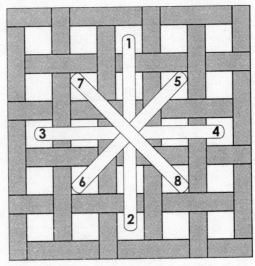

Star Stitch

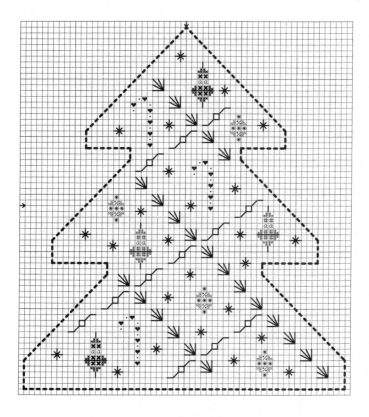